Rafe's Gaze Was Locked On The Empty Doorway Where Katie Had Been Standing Only A Moment Before.

The guys had been joking with him because they could, and Rafe would take it because it was all part of the bet he'd lost. Good-natured teasing and joking around was all part of working a job. But Katie's defense of him had surprised him. Hell, he couldn't even remember the last time someone had stood up for him—not counting his half brothers and cousins.

Katie Charles was like no one he'd ever met before. She didn't want anything from him. Wasn't trying to get on his good side. But then, that was because she thought he was just an ordinary man.

It would be an entirely different story if she knew he was a King.

Dear Reader,

Everyone always asks a writer where she gets her ideas. Well, the idea for this book wasn't hard to come by!

My husband and I lived through a kitchen remodel this year—and I just knew that it would make a great background for a Kings of California novel.

So, meet Rafe King. He's one of three brothers who own King Construction. He's lost a bet and for the first time in years, he has to actually work at a job site. But to keep from intimidating his own employees, Rafe goes undercover as Rafe Cole.

Now, meet Katie Charles, the Cookie Queen. Katie's having her kitchen remodeled. She's not a big fan of the Kings, though, because one of those King cousins broke her heart. Right off the bat, she tells Rafe she has no use for the King men.

And that's a challenge Rafe simply can't ignore.

I hope you have as much fun reading this story as I did writing it. And only a couple of the kitchen "incidents" are torn from real life!

Please visit my website at www.maureenchild.com or write to me in care of Harlequin Books Reader Services. I love hearing from you.

Happy reading,

Maureen

MAUREEN CHILD

KING'S MILLION-DOLLAR SECRET

Recycling programs
for this product may
not exist in your area.

ISBN-13: 978-0-373-73096-4

KING'S MILLION-DOLLAR SECRET

www.Harlequin.com

Printed in U.S.A.

Books by Maureen Child

Desire

MAUREEN CHILD

is a California native who loves to travel. Every chance they get, she and her husband are taking off on another research trip. The author of more than sixty books, Maureen loves a happy ending and still swears that she has the best job in the world. She lives in Southern California with her husband, two children and a golden retriever with delusions of grandeur. Visit Maureen's website at www.maureenchild.com.

To Rory, Scott and Joaquin
at Building and Construction Contractors,
the heroes who rebuilt my kitchen,
put up with my constant questions
and made a palace out of a pup tent!

Thanks, you guys.

One

Rafe King liked a friendly wager as much as the next guy.

He just didn't like to lose.

When he lost though, he paid up. Which was why he was standing in a driveway, sipping a cup of coffee, waiting for the rest of the work crew to show up. As one of the owners of King Construction, it had been a few years since Rafe had actually done any on-site work. Usually, he was the details man, getting parts ordered, supplies delivered. He stayed on top of the million and one jobs the company had going at any one time and trusted the contractors to get the work done right.

Now though, thanks to one bet gone bad, he'd be working on this job himself for the next few weeks.

A silver pickup truck towing a small, enclosed trailer pulled in behind him and Rafe slanted his gaze at the driver. Joe Hanna. Contractor. Friend. And the man who'd instigated the bet Rafe had lost.

Joe climbed out of his truck, barely managing to hide a smile. "Hardly knew you without the suit you're usually wearing."

"Funny." Most of his life, Rafe hadn't done the suit thing. Actually, he was more comfortable dressed as he was now, in faded jeans, black work boots and a black T-shirt with King Construction stamped across the back. "You're late."

"No, I'm not. You're early." Joe sipped at his own coffee and handed over a bag. "Want a doughnut?"

"Sure." Rafe dug in, came up with a jelly-filled and polished it off in a few huge bites. "Where's everyone else?"

"We don't start work until eight a.m. They've still got a half hour."

"If they were here now, they could start setting up, so they could start working at eight." Rafe turned his gaze to the California bungalow that would be the center of his world for the next several weeks. It sat on a tree-lined street in Long Beach, behind a wide, neatly tended lawn. At least fifty years old, it looked settled, he supposed. As if the town had grown up around it.

"What's the job here, anyway?"

"A kitchen redo," Joe said, leaning against Rafe's truck to study the house. "New floor, new counter. Lots of plumbing to bring the old place up to code. New drains, pipes, replastering and painting."

"Cabinets?" Rafe asked, his mind fixing on the job at hand.

"Nope. The ones in there are solid white pine. So we're not replacing. Just stripping, sanding and varnishing."

He nodded, then straightened up and turned his gaze on Joe. "So do the guys working this job know who I am?"

Joe grinned. "Not a clue. Just like we talked about, your real identity will be a secret. For the length of the job here, your name is Rafe Cole. You're a new hire."

Better all the way around, he thought, if the guys working with him didn't know that *he* was their employer. If they knew the truth, they'd be antsy and wouldn't get the work done. Besides, this was an opportunity for Rafe to see exactly what his employees thought of the business and working for King Construction. Like that television show where employers went undercover at their own companies, he just might find out a few things.

Still, he shook his head. "Remind me again why I'm not firing you?"

"Because you lost the bet fair and square and you don't welsh on your bets," Joe said. "And, I warned you that my Sherry's car was going to win the race."

"True." Rafe smiled and remembered the scene at the King Construction family picnic a month ago. The children of employees spent months building cars that would then race on a track made especially for the event. In the spirit of competition, Rafe had bet against Joe's daughter's bright pink car. Sherry had left everyone else standing at the gate. That would teach him to bet against a female.

"Good thing you let your brothers do all the talking at the picnic," Joe was saying. "Otherwise, these guys would recognize you."

That's just the way Rafe liked it, he thought. He left the publicity and the more public areas of the business to two of his brothers, Sean and Lucas. Between the three of them, they had built King Construction into the biggest construction firm on the West Coast. Sean handled the corporate side of things, Lucas managed the customer base and crews, and Rafe was the go-to guy for supplies, parts and anything else needed on a site.

"Lucky me," he muttered, then looked up at the rumble of another truck pulling up to the front of the house. Right behind him, a smaller truck parked and the two men got out and walked toward them.

Joe stepped up. "Steve, Arturo, this is Rafe Cole. He'll be working the job with you guys."

Steve was tall, about fifty, with a wide grin, wearing a T-shirt proclaiming a local rock band. Arturo was older, shorter and wearing a shirt stained with various colors of paint. Well, Rafe thought, he knew which one of them was the painter.

"We ready?" Steve asked.

"As we'll ever be." Joe turned and pointed to the side of the house. "There's an RV access gate there. Want to put the trailer in her back yard? Easier to get to and it'll keep thieves out."

"Right."

Joe positioned his truck and trailer through the gate and in minutes, they were busy. Rafe jumped in. It had been a few years since he'd spent time on a site, but that didn't mean he'd forgotten anything. His father, Ben King, hadn't been much of a dad, but he had run the construction arm of the King family dynasty and made sure that every one of his sons—all eight of them—spent time on job sites every summer. He figured it was a good way to remind them that being a King didn't mean you had an easy ride.

They'd all grumbled about it at the time, but Rafe had

come to think that was the one good thing their father had done for any of them.

"We did the walk-through last week," Joe was saying and Rafe listened up. "The customer's got everything cleaned out, so Steve and Arturo can start the demo right away. Rafe, you're going to hook up a temporary cooking station for Ms. Charles on her enclosed patio."

Rafe just looked at him. "Temporary cooking? She can't eat out during a kitchen rehab like everyone else?"

"She could," a female voice answered from the house behind them. "But she needs to be able to bake while you're fixing her kitchen."

Rafe slowly turned to face the woman behind that voice and felt a hard punch of something hot slam into him. She was tall, which he liked—nothing worse than having to hunch over to kiss a woman—she had curly, shoulder-length red hair and bright green eyes. She was smiling and the curve of her mouth was downright delectable.

And none of that information made him happy. He didn't need a woman. Didn't want a woman and if he did, he sure as hell wouldn't be going for one who had "white picket fences" practically stamped on her forehead.

Rafe just wasn't the home-and-hearth kind of guy.

Still, that didn't mean he couldn't enjoy the view.

"Morning, Ms. Charles," Joe said. "Got your crew here. Arturo and Steve you met the other day during the walk-through. And this is Rafe."

"Nice to meet you," she said. Her green eyes locked with his and for one long, humming second there seemed to be a hell of a lot of heat in the air. "But call me Katie, please. We're going to be spending a lot of time together, after all."

"Right. So, what's this temporary cooking station about?" Rafe asked.

"I bake cookies," she told him. "That's my business and I have to be able to fill orders while the kitchen is being redone. Joe assured me it wouldn't be a problem."

"It won't be," Joe said. "Of course, you won't be able to cook during the day. We'll have the gas turned off while we work on the pipes. But we'll set it up for you at the end of every day. Rafe'll fix you up and you'll be cooking by tonight."

"Great. Well, I'll let you get to it."

She slipped inside again and Rafe took that second to admire the view of her from the rear. She had a great behind, hugged by worn denim that defined every curve and tempted a man to see what exactly was underneath those jeans. He took a long, deep breath, hoping the crisp morning air would dissipate some of the heat pumping through him. It didn't, so he was left with a too-tight body and a long day staring him in the face. So he told himself to ignore the woman. He was only here long enough to pay off a bet. Then he'd be gone.

"Okay," Joe was saying, "you guys move Katie's stove where she wants it, then Rafe can get her set up while the demolition's going on."

Nothing Rafe would like better than to set her up—for some one-on-one time. Instead though, he followed Steve and Arturo around to the back of the house.

The noise was incredible.

After an hour, Katie's head was pounding in time with the sledge hammers being swung in her grandmother's kitchen.

It was weird, having strangers in the house. Even

weirder paying them to destroy the kitchen she'd pretty much grown up in. But it would all be worth it, she knew. She just hoped she could live through the construction.

Not to mention crabby carpenters.

Desperate to get a little distance between herself and the constant battering of noise, she walked to the enclosed patio. Snugged between the garage and the house, the room was long and narrow. There were a few chairs, a picnic table that Katie had already covered with a vinyl tablecloth and stacks of cookie sheets waiting to be filled. Her mixing bowls were on a nearby counter and her temporary pantry was a card table. This was going to be a challenge for sure. But there was the added plus of having a gorgeous man stretched out behind the stove grumbling under his breath.

"How's it going?" she asked.

The man jerked up, slammed his head into the corner of the stove and muttered an oath that Katie was glad she hadn't been able to hear. Flashing her a dark look out of beautiful blue eyes, he said, "It's going as well as hooking up an ancient stove to a gas pipe can go."

"It's old, but it's reliable," Katie told him. "Of course, I've got a new one on order."

"Can't say as I blame you," Rafe answered, dipping back behind the stove again. "This thing's gotta be thirty years old."

"At least," she said, dropping into a nearby chair. "My grandmother bought it new before I was born and I'm twenty-seven."

He glanced up at her and shook his head.

Her breath caught in her chest. Really, he was not what she had expected. Someone as gorgeous as he was should have been on the cover of *GQ*, not working a construction site. But he seemed to know what he was doing and she had to admit that just looking at him gave her the kind of rush she hadn't felt in way too long.

And that kind of thinking was just dangerous, so she steered the conversation to something light.

"Just because something's old doesn't mean it's useless." She grinned. "That stove might be temperamental, but I know all of its tricks. It cooks a little hot, but I've learned to work around it."

"And yet," he pointed out with a half smile, "you've got a new stove coming."

She shrugged and her smile faded a little into something that felt like regret. "New kitchen, new stove. But I think I'll miss this one's occasional hiccups. Makes baking more interesting."

"Right." He looked as if he didn't believe her and couldn't have cared less. "You're really going to be cooking out here?"

The sounds of cheerful demolition rang out around them and Katie heard the two guys in the kitchen laughing about something. She wondered for a second or two what could possibly be funny about tearing out a fifty-year-old kitchen, then told herself it was probably better if she didn't know.

Instead, she glanced around at the patio/makeshift kitchen setup. Windows ringed the room, terra-cotta-colored tiles made up the floor and there was a small wetbar area in the corner that Katie would be using as a cleanup area. She sighed a little, already missing the farmhouse-style kitchen that was, at the moment, being taken down to its skeleton.

But when it was finished, she'd have the kitchen of her dreams. She smiled to herself, enjoying the mental images.

"Something funny?"

"What?" She looked at the man still sprawled on the tile floor. "No. Just thinking about how the kitchen will be when you guys are done."

"Not worried about the mess and the work?"

"Nope," she said and pushed out of the chair. She walked toward him, leaned on the stove top and looked over the back at him. "Oh, don't get me wrong. I'm not looking forward to it and the thought of baking out here is a little high on the ye gods scale. Still, the mess can't be avoided," she said. "As for the work that will be done, I did my research. Checked into all the different construction companies and got three estimates."

"So, why'd you choose King Construction?" he asked, dragging what looked like a silver snake from the back of the stove to a pipe jutting out from the garage wall.

"It wasn't easy," she murmured, remembering things she would just as soon put behind her permanently.

"Why's that?" He sounded almost offended. "King Construction has a great reputation."

Katie smiled and said, "It's nice that you're so protective of the company you work for."

"Yeah, well. The Kings have been good to me." He scowled a bit and refocused on the task at hand. "So if you don't like King Construction, what're we doing here?"

Sighing a little, Katie told herself she really had to be more discreet. She hadn't meant to say anything at all about the King family. After all, Rafe and the other guys worked for them. But now that she had, she wasn't going to try to lie or squirm her way out of it, either. "I'm sure the construction company is excellent. All of the referrals I checked out were more than pleased with the work done."

"But…?" He patted the wall, stood up and looked at her, waiting for her to finish.

Katie straightened up as he did and noticed that though she was five foot nine, he had at least four inches on her. He also had the palest blue eyes she had ever seen, fringed by thick eyelashes that most women would kill for. His black eyebrows looked as though they were always drawn into a frown. His mouth was full and tempting and his jaws were covered with just the slightest hint of black stubble. His shoulders were broad, his waist narrow and those jeans of his really did look amazingly good on him. A fresh tingle of interest swept through her almost before she realized it.

It was nice to feel something for an ordinary, everyday, hard-working guy. She'd had enough of rich men with more money than sense or manners.

He was still waiting, so she gave him a bright smile and said, "Let's just say it's a personal matter between me and one member of the King family."

If anything, the perpetual scowl on his face deepened. "What do you mean?"

"It's not important." She shook her head and laughed. "Honestly, I'm sorry I said anything. I only meant that it was hard for me to hire King Construction, knowing what I do about the King family men."

"Really." He folded his arms over his chest and asked, "What exactly do you think you know about the Kings?"

His gaze was narrowed and fixed on her. She felt the power of that glare right down to her bones and even Katie was surprised at the tingle of something tempting washing through her. Suddenly nervous, she glanced over the back of the stove to look at the pipes as if she knew what she was seeing. Still, it gave her a second to gather her thoughts. When she felt steady again, she said, "You mean beside the fact that they're too rich and too snobby?"

"Snobby?"

"Yes." Katie huffed out a breath and said, "Look I know you work for them and I don't want to make you uncomfortable. I only know that I never want anything to do with any of them again."

"Sounds ominous."

She laughed at the idea. Katie doubted very much that Cordell King had given her a second thought since he'd abruptly disappeared from her life six months ago. No, the Kings steamrolled their way through the world, expecting everyone else to get out of their way. Well, from now on, she was going to oblige them.

"Oh, I don't think any of the Kings of California are staying up nights wondering why Katie Charles hates their guts."

"You might be surprised," he said, dusting his hands off as he looked at her. She shifted a little under that direct stare. "You know, I'm a curious kind of guy. And I'm not going to be happy until I know why you hate the Kings."

"Curiosity isn't always a good thing," she said. "Sometimes you find out things you'd rather not know."

"Better to be informed anyway, don't you think?"

"Not always," Katie said, remembering how badly she'd felt when Cordell broke things off with her. She'd just had to ask him *why* and the answer had only made her feel worse.

Rafe smiled at her then and she noted how his features softened and even his eyes lost that cool, dispassionate gleam. Her heartbeat jittered unsteadily in her chest as her body reacted to the man's pure male appeal. Then, as if he knew exactly what she was thinking, that smile of his widened and he actually *winked* at her.

But a moment later, he was all business again.

"Your temporary gas line is hooked up. But remember, we're shutting the gas off during the day. We'll let you know when it's safe to use the stove."

"Okay. Thanks." She took a single step backward and Rafe walked past her, his arm brushing against hers as he did. Heat flashed through her unexpectedly and Katie took in a deep breath. Unfortunately, that meant she also got a good long whiff of his cologne. Something foresty and cool and almost as intriguing as the man himself. "And Rafe?"

"Yeah?"

"Please don't repeat any of what I said about the King family. I mean, I probably shouldn't have brought it up and I don't want to make anyone uncomfortable while you're working here."

He nodded. "Won't say a word. But like I said, one of these days, I'm going to hear the rest of your story."

Katie shook her head and said, "I don't think so. The Kings are part of my past and that's where I want to leave them."

By the end of the first day, Katie was asking herself why she had ever decided to remodel. Having strangers in and out of her house all day was weird, having *noisy* strangers only made it worse.

Now though, they were gone and she was left alone in the shell of what had been her grandmother's kitchen. Standing in the center of the room, she did a slow circle, her gaze moving over everything.

The floor had been torn up, right down to the black

subfloor that was older than Katie. The walls were half
torn down and the cabinet doors had been removed and
stacked neatly in the back yard. She caught a glimpse
of naked pipes and groaned in sympathy with the old
house.

"Regrets?"

She jumped and whirled around. Her heart jolted into
a gallop even as she blew out a relieved breath. "Rafe.
I thought you left with the others."

He grinned as if he knew that he'd startled her. Then,
leaning one shoulder on the doorjamb, he folded his
arms across his chest. "I stayed to make sure your gas
hookup in the back room was working."

"And is it?"

"All set."

"Thanks. I appreciate it."

He shrugged and straightened up languidly as if he
had all the time in the world. "It's my job."

"I know, but I appreciate it anyway."

"You're welcome." His gaze moved over the room as
hers had a moment before. "So, what do you think?"

"Honestly?" She cringed a little. "It's horrifying."

He laughed. "Just remember. Destruction first. Then
creation."

"I'll try to remember." She walked closer to where the
sink had been. Now, of course, it was just a ripped-out
wall with those naked pipes staring at her in accusation.
"Hard to believe the room can come back from this."

"I've seen worse."

"I don't know whether to be relieved or appalled at
that statement," she admitted.

"Go with relieved," he assured her. He walked closer,
stuffing his hands into the back pockets of his jeans.
"Some of the jobs I've seen took *months* to finish."

"So you've done a lot of this work?"

"My share," he said with a shrug. "Though this is the first job site I've worked on in three or four years."

The house was quiet…blessedly so, after a full day of hammers crashing into walls and wood. The decimated kitchen echoed with their voices, and outside, the afternoon was fading into twilight. There was a feeling of intimacy between them that maybe only strangers thrown together could experience.

She looked at him, taking her time to enjoy the view, and wondered. About him. About who he was, what he liked—and a part of her wondered why she wondered.

Then again, it had been a long time since she'd been interested in a man. Having your heart bruised was enough to make a woman just a little nervous about getting back into the dating pool again.

But it couldn't hurt to *look,* could it?

"So if you weren't doing construction, what were you doing instead?"

He glanced at her, long enough for her to see a mental shutter slam down across his eyes. Then he shifted his gaze away and ran one hand across the skeleton of a cabinet. "Different things. Still, good to get back and work with my hands again." Then he winked. "Even if it *is* for the Kings."

He'd shut her out deliberately. Closing the door on talking about his past. He was watching her as if he expected her to dig a little deeper. But how could she? She had already told him that she felt curiosity was overrated. And if she asked about his past, didn't that give him the right to ask about hers? Katie didn't exactly want to chat about how she'd been wined, dined and then unceremoniously dumped by Cordell King either, did she?

Still, she couldn't help being curious about Rafe Cole and just what he might be hiding.

"So," he said after a long moment of silence stretched out between them. "Guess I'd better get going and let you get busy baking cookies."

"Right." She started forward at the same time he did and they bumped into each other.

Instantly, heat blossomed between them. Their bodies close together, there was one incredible, sizzling moment in which neither of them spoke because they simply didn't have to.

Something was there. Heat. Passion.

Katie looked up into Rafe's eyes and knew he was feeling exactly what she was. And judging by his expression, he wasn't much happier about it.

She hadn't been looking for a romantic connection, but it seemed that she had stumbled on one anyway.

He lifted one hand to touch her face and stopped himself just short of his fingertips tracing along her jaw. Smiling softly, he said, "This could get...interesting."

Understatement of the century.

Two

"Meeting's over," Lucas King muttered. "Why are we still here?"

"Because I've got a question for you," Rafe answered and looked up at his brothers. Well, two of them, anyway. Sean and Lucas, his partners in King Construction. Just looking at the three of them together, anyone would know they were brothers. They all had the King coloring, black hair and blue eyes. Yet their features were different enough to point to the fact that they each had different mothers.

But the man who had been their father had linked them not just by blood, but by fostering that brotherly connection in their childhoods. All of Ben King's sons had spent time together every summer, and the differences among them melted away in the shared knowledge that their father hadn't bothered to marry *any* of their mothers.

Lucas, the oldest of the three of them, was checking his watch and firing another impatient look at Rafe. Sean, typically, was so busy studying the screen of his cell phone while he tapped out messages to God knew who, he hadn't noticed that Lucas had spoken.

The brothers held weekly meetings to discuss business, to catch up with whatever was going on in the family and simply to keep up with each other's lives. Those meetings shifted among each of their houses. Tonight, they were gathered at Lucas's oceanfront home in Long Beach.

It was huge, old and filled with what Lucas liked to call character. Of course, everyone else called it outdated and inconvenient. Rafe preferred his own place, a penthouse suite in a hotel in Huntington Beach. Sleek, modern and efficient, it had none of the quirks that Lucas seemed so fond of in his own house. And he appreciated having room service at his beck and call as well as maid service every day. As for Sean, he was living in a remodeled water tower in Sunset Beach that had an elevator at beach level just to get you to the front door.

They had wildly different tastes, yet each of them had opted for a home with a view of the sea.

For a moment, Rafe stared out at the ribbons of color on the sunset-stained ocean and took a deep breath of the cold, clear air. There were a few hardy surfers astride their boards, looking for one last wave before calling it a day, and a couple was walking a tiny dog along Pacific Coast Highway.

"What do we know about Katie Charles?" he asked, taking a swig from his beer.

"Katie who?" Sean asked.

"Charles," Lucas said, irritation for their younger brother coloring his tone. "Don't you listen?"

"To who?" Sean kept his gaze fixed on his cell phone. The man was forever emailing and texting clients and women. It was nearly impossible to get Sean to pay attention to anything that didn't pop up on an LED screen.

"Me," Rafe told him, reaching out to snatch the phone away.

"Hey!" Sean leaned out and reclaimed his phone. "I'm setting up a meeting for later."

"How about instead you pay attention to *this* one?" Rafe countered.

"Fine. I'm listening. Give me my phone."

Rafe tossed it over, then turned his gaze to Lucas. "So?" Rafe asked. "You know anything about Katie Charles?"

"Name sounds familiar. Who is she?"

"Customer," Rafe said, picking up his beer and leaning back in the Adirondack chair. "We're redoing her kitchen."

"Good for us." Sean looked at him. "So what's bugging you about her?"

Good question. Rafe shouldn't have cared what Katie Charles thought of the King family. What did it really matter in the grand scheme of things? Still, ever since leaving Katie's house earlier, he hadn't been able to stop thinking about her. And it wasn't just the flash of heat he felt when he was around her that was bugging her. She was pretty, smart, and successful, and she hated the Kings. What was up with that?

"Katie Charles," Lucas was muttering to himself. "Katie Charles. Kitchen. Cookies." He grinned and said, "That's it. Katie's Kookies. She's building a real name for herself. She's sort of a cottage industry at the moment, but people are talking about her."

"What people?" Rafe asked, frowning. "I've never heard of her before."

Sean snorted. "Why would you? You're practically a hermit. To hear about anything you'd have to actually talk to someone. You know, someone who isn't *us*."

"I'm not a hermit."

"God knows I hate to admit Sean's right. About anything. But he's got a point," Lucas said, stretching his long legs out in front of him. "You keep yourself shut up in that penthouse of yours most of the time. Hell, I'm willing to bet the only people you've actually talked to since last week's meeting are the room service operator and the crew you worked with today."

Rafe scowled at Lucas, but only because he didn't have an argument for the truth. He didn't have time to date every model in the known universe like Sean. And he had no interest in the corporate world of movers and shakers like Lucas. What the hell else was he supposed to do with his time?

"Oh, yeah," Sean said with a grin. "I forgot about that bet you made. How's it going, being back on a job site?"

"Not bad," Rafe admitted. Actually, he'd enjoyed himself more than he had expected. Being on a site with hardworking guys who didn't know he was their boss had been…fun. And there was the added plus of being around a woman who made his body tight and his brain fuzz out. Until, of course, Katie had confessed that she hated the King family.

"So," Sean asked, "if you had such a good time, why do you look like you want to bite through a box of nails?"

"You do look more annoyed than usual," Lucas said with a shrug. "What's up? And what's it got to do with Katie Charles?"

"Neither of you knows her?"

Sean and Lucas looked at each other and shrugged. "Nope."

"Somebody does."

"Somebody knows everybody," Lucas pointed out.

"Yeah, but the somebody who knows Katie is a King."

Sean snorted. "Doesn't narrow the field down by much."

"True." Hell, there were so many King cousins in California, they could probably start their own county.

"What's the deal?" Lucas picked up his beer, leaned back in his chair and waited. "Why's she bothering you?"

"Because," Rafe told him, standing up to walk to the balcony railing, "she hates the Kings."

"Hates us?" Sean laughed. "Impossible. Women *love* King men."

"That's completely true," Lucas said with a self-satisfied smile.

"Usually, maybe," Rafe said, his gaze sweeping across the froth of waves on the darkening ocean. Although his ex-wife would probably argue that point. "But this woman doesn't. Hell she barely could say the word *King* without shuddering."

"So why'd she hire us if she hates us so much?"

He turned to look at Sean. "Our company's reputation, she says. But she's not happy about it."

"And you think somebody in the family turned her against all Kings?" Lucas asked.

"What else could it be?" Rafe looked at him and shrugged.

"The real question here is," Sean said quietly, "why do you care?"

"That is a good question." Lucas looked at Rafe and waited.

Too good, Rafe thought. Hell, he didn't know why he cared, either. God knew, he didn't want to. He'd been down this road before and he'd already learned that not only didn't he know how to love, but according to his ex-wife, he was actually *incapable* of it.

So why bother with romancing a woman when you knew going in it was doomed to fail? No, he kept his relationships easy. Uncomplicated. A few hours of recreational sex and no strings attached.

Better for everyone when the rules were clear.

Yet, there was Katie.

She stirred him up in a way he'd never known before, though damned if he'd admit that to anyone else. Hard enough to get himself to acknowledge it.

"Yeah, it is a good question," Rafe muttered. "Too bad I don't have an answer."

Katie was getting used to the noise, the dust, the confusion and the presence of strangers in her house. One week and she could barely remember what quiet was like. Or privacy. Or being able to move around her kitchen to the sounds of late-night radio.

Now, her kitchen was an empty shell of a room. She glanced out one of the wide windows into the backyard and sighed. There was a small trailer parked on her grass, its doors wide open, revealing tools and equipment enough to build four kitchens.

Pickup trucks belonging to Steve, Arturo and Rafe

were also parked on her lawn and the piles of her discarded kitchen were getting bigger. Broken linoleum, old pipes, her *sink*—a beautiful, cast iron relic—lay tilted atop one of the mountains of trash and just for a second, Katie felt a twinge of panic.

This had all seemed like such a good idea at the time. Now though, she had to wonder if she'd been crazy. What if the new kitchen wasn't as good as the old? What if her new stove didn't cook as reliably? Where would she ever find another sink so wide and deep? What if her business went belly up and she'd spent her savings on a kitchen she wouldn't be able to afford?

"Oh, God…"

"Too late for panic now," a deep voice assured her from the doorway.

She turned around to look at Rafe and caught the knowing gleam in his eyes. She forced a smile. "Not full-blown panic yet. Just a little…okay," she admitted finally, "panic."

He laughed and she had a moment to think how devastating he really was before the smile on his face faded. He walked into the room and looked out at the view she'd been staring at. "It looks bad now, but it's going to be great when it's finished."

"Easy for you to say."

"Yeah, it is. This isn't my first rodeo, you know. I've done a lot of remodels and the owners always have that wild-eyed look you have right now." He lifted one shoulder in a shrug. "But they're always happy when it's over."

"Because it's over or because they love what you did to their houses?"

"A little of both, maybe," he acknowledged. "Just

wanted to let you know we found a leak in a hot-water pipe."

"A *leak?*" Katie instantly had mental images of a rising flood beneath the house.

"Relax," he said. "It's just an old, slow leak. The joint on the pipes is bad. We're going to replace it, we just need to show it to you first and get you to sign off on the work, since it's extra to the contract."

She blew out a relieved breath. "Right. Okay then. Lead the way."

Katie followed Rafe out of the patio, across the yard and through the back door to the kitchen. She couldn't even reach her favorite room in the old house by walking down the hallway. It was crowded with her refrigerator, tables holding all of her pantry items and towers of pots and pans.

The sun was blazing down out of a clear blue sky and she was grateful for California weather. If she'd had to do this remodeling job in a place renowned for rain, it would have been far worse.

Rafe held the door open for her and she walked inside to a room she barely recognized. The old subfloor was black and littered with dust. The skeletons of the cabinets stood out like picked over bones on the walls. The pipes looked forlorn somehow, as if they were embarrassed to be seen.

Steve, the plumber, was crawling up out of a hole in the floor. Katie just managed to hide a shudder. You couldn't pay her enough to crawl under the house where spiders and God knew what other kind of bug lived. When he was clear, Steve turned to flash her a smile. "If you come over here, I can show you the leak."

"Great. Leaks." She picked her way across the floor, stepping over scattered tools and bits of old wood. She stopped alongside the long, narrow opening in the floor and squatted beside Steve. He held a flashlight pointed beneath the floorboards and said, "There it is. Probably been dripping like that for years. Hasn't done any damage, so that's good. But we should put in a new copper joint."

Katie nodded solemnly as if she understood exactly what he was talking about. But the truth was, she didn't see a leak. All she noticed was a damp spot on the earth beneath the floor that probably shouldn't be there. If she actually admitted she couldn't see the leak, they might insist she go down there to see it up close and personal. So Steve's word would be good enough for her. "Okay then. Do what you have to."

"Excellent." Steve turned and said, "Hey, Rafe, why don't you show her the new sink you brought in this morning."

"My new sink's here? Already?" Now this she was interested in. As far as pipes went, all she cared about was that they carried water whichever way they were designed to carry it without leaks, thanks very much. She didn't need to understand how they did it. Hard to get thrilled over copper piping.

"I was at one of our suppliers and saw a sink I thought you'd like, so I picked it up. We'll just store it in the trailer until it's time to install." Rafe led her out of the kitchen, down the back steps and across the lawn.

Arturo had the cabinet doors spread across makeshift sawhorse work tables and was busily scraping off the old finish before sanding them. Everything was happening. Only a week and already she was seeing progress. Maybe they'd get it all done in two weeks, Katie thought, then smiled wryly to herself. And maybe she'd sprout wings and fly.

"Here it is." Rafe stopped at the trailer, reached in and drew out a huge sink, one side much deeper and bigger than the other.

"Isn't that heavy?" she asked, remembering the loud *clunk* her old cast-iron sink had made when tossed to the top of the junk pile.

"Nope. It's acrylic." He held it in one hand to prove his point. "Tougher and won't chip or rust."

She smoothed her fingers over the edge and sighed a little. It was perfect. Looking up at him, she said, "Thank you. It's great."

"Glad you like it." He tucked it back into the trailer and draped a protective work blanket over it.

"I thought the contractor was supposed to pick up the supplies for the job," she said.

He turned back to look at her and shoved both hands into the pockets of his jeans. "Joe asked me to pick up a few things at the home store. I saw the sink and…"

"How'd you know I'd like it?"

"Took a shot," he admitted.

"It was a good one."

His blue eyes were shining and a cool wind tossed his black hair across his forehead. He was tall, broad-shouldered and looked *great* in those faded jeans, she thought, not for the first time. In fact, she had dreamed about him the night before. In her dream they were back in her kitchen, alone, as they had been yesterday. But in her fantasy, Rafe had kissed her until her toes curled and she had awakened so taut with desire and tension she hadn't been able to go back to sleep.

Even her unconscious mind was working against her.

"So, Rafe Cole," she asked, "how long have you been in construction?"

She thought his features tightened briefly, but the expression was gone so quickly, she couldn't be sure. Now why would that simple question get such a reaction?

"My dad started me out in the business when I was a kid," he said, staring off at the house, keeping his gaze deliberately away from hers. "I liked it and just sort of stuck with it."

"I get that," she said, trying to put him at ease again, to regain the easiness they'd shared only a moment ago. "My grandmother started me out baking when I was a little girl, and, well, here I am."

He nodded and glanced at her. "How long have you lived here?"

"I grew up here," she said. "My dad died before I was born, and my mom and I moved in here with Nana." Her gaze tracked across the familiar lines of the old bungalow. The windows were wide, the roof was shake and the paint was peeling in spots. But the house was home. It meant security. Comfort. "I moved out for college, then mom died and a year ago, I inherited the house from Nana."

"Oh," he said softly. "I'm sorry."

It took her a second; then Katie laughed and told him, "No, she didn't die. She just moved. Nana and her sister Grace decided to share an apartment at the Senior Living Center. They figure there are lots of lonely men over there looking for love!"

He laughed at that and once again, Katie felt a rush of something hot and delicious spread through her. The man should smile more often, she thought and wondered why he didn't. The other guys working here were forever laughing and joking around. But not Rafe.

He was more quiet. More mysterious.

Just…*more*.

Rafe sat opposite his brother Sean at a local diner and waited for his burger. As for Sean, he was typing out a message or thirty on his cell phone. Okay, as far as Rafe was concerned. Gave him more time to think about Katie Charles.

The woman was haunting him.

He couldn't remember being so fixated on a single woman—not even Leslie, before he married her, had so completely captivated him. While that should have worried him, instead he was intrigued. What was it about Katie that was getting to him?

She was beautiful, sure. But lots of women were. He wanted her, but he had *wanted* lots of women. There was something else about her that was reaching out to him on so many different levels, he couldn't even name them all.

"Hey," Sean said with a laugh. "Where'd you go?"

"What?" Rafe swiveled on the bench seat and looked at his younger brother.

"I've been talking to you for five minutes and you haven't heard a word. So I was wondering just what exactly had you thinking so hard."

Rafe scowled a little, irritated to have been caught daydreaming. Jeez. Thoughts of Katie were taking up way too much of his time. "Not surprising I was thinking of something else, since you were so busy texting."

"Nice try," Sean said, still grinning. "Distract me with insults so I won't ask if you're still thinking about the cookie woman."

Rafe shot him a glare. "Her name's Katie."

"Yeah, I know."

"Anyone ever tell you how irritating you are?"

"Besides you, you mean?" Sean asked, giving their waitress a bright smile as she delivered their dinners. "You bet. All the time."

Rafe had to smile. Sean was absolutely the most laid-back King ever born. Most of them were type A's, ruthlessly pushing through life, demanding and getting their own way. Not Sean. He had a way of slipping up on whatever he wanted until it just naturally fell into his hands.

He was damn hard to annoy and almost never lost his temper. In the world of the King family, he was an original.

Once the waitress was gone, the brothers dove into their meals. This hamburger joint on Ocean Avenue had been a popular spot since the forties. Rafe and Sean were on the outside patio, where they could watch traffic and pedestrians in a never-ending stream of motion. Kids, dogs, parents with digital cameras poking out of their pockets fought for space on the crowded sidewalk. Summer in a beach town brought out the tourists.

"So," Sean said, reaching for his beer, "let's hear it."

"Hear what?"

"About the cookie lady," Sean countered, both of his eyebrows wiggling.

Rafe sighed. Should have expected that his brother would be curious. After all, Rafe hadn't talked about a woman since Leslie walked out. He remembered his ex-wife looking at him sadly and telling him that she felt "sorry" for him because he had no idea how to love someone. That he never should have married her and sentenced her to a cold, empty life.

Then he thought about Katie and it was like a

cool, soft breeze wafted through his mind. "She's…
different."

"This gets better and better." Sean leaned back in his
booth and waited.

Frowning, Rafe took a sip of his beer. When he spoke,
it was a warning not only to his brother, but to himself.
"Don't make more of this than there is. I just find her
interesting."

"Interesting." Sean nodded. "Right. Like a bug
collection?"

"What?"

Laughing, his brother said, "Come off it, Rafe. There's
something there and you're looking. And about time too,
I want to say. Leslie was a long time ago, man."

"Not that long," Rafe countered. Although, as he
thought about it, he realized that he and Leslie had been
divorced for more than five years. His ex-wife was now
remarried to Rafe's former best friend, with a set of
toddler twins and a newborn, last he heard.

"Long enough for her to move on. Why haven't
you?"

Rafe shot Sean a glare that should have fried his
ass on the spot. Typically enough though, Sean wasn't
bothered. "Who says I haven't?"

"Me. Lucas. Tanner. Mac. Grady…" Sean stopped,
paused and asked, "Do I have to name *all* of our brothers
or do you get the point?"

"I get it, but you're wrong." Rafe took a bite of his
truly excellent burger and after chewing, added, "I'm
not carrying a torch for Leslie. It's over. Done. She's a
mother, for God's sake." And if he was to be honest, he
hadn't really missed her when she left. So what did that
say about him?

"Yet, you're still living in a hotel suite making do with the occasional date with a beautiful airhead."

"I like living in a hotel and they're not all airheads."

"Good argument."

"Look," Rafe said, reaching for his beer. "Katie's a nice woman, but she's off limits."

"Why's that?"

"Because she's got white picket fence written all over her," Rafe explained. "She's the settle-down-and-get-married type and I've already proven I'm not."

Sean shook his head and sighed. "For a smart guy, you're not real bright, are you?"

"Thanks for the support."

"You want support?" Sean asked, digging into his burger. "Then stop being an idiot."

"Shut up. I tried the happily-ever-after thing and it blew up in my face. Not going to do it again."

"Did you ever consider that maybe the reason it didn't work was because you married the wrong woman?"

Rafe didn't even bother answering that jibe. What would have been the point?

Monday morning, the guys were still fighting with the pipes and Katie was ready for a week in Tahiti. She'd hardly slept all weekend. Though the peace and quiet were great, she'd been so busy filling cookie orders she hadn't had time to appreciate it.

Now she sipped at a cup of coffee and winced every time the whine of a drill shrieked into the air.

"The noise is worst the first week," someone from nearby said.

She turned to look at Joe Hanna, the contractor. "You're just saying that so I won't run away."

He grinned. "Once the new pipes and drains are

installed, the rest will be easier for you to live with. I promise."

He had no sooner made that vow when a shout came from the kitchen. "Arturo! Shut off the water! Off! Off!"

"Crap." Joe hustled across the yard just behind Rafe while Arturo sprinted for the water shutoff valve out front. Katie was hot on Joe's heels and stepped into the kitchen in time to see Steve crouched over a pipe with water spraying out of it like a fountain in Vegas.

Katie backed out of their way while the men grabbed towels. Then Arturo got the water off and the three men in the kitchen were left standing around as what looked like the incoming tide rolled across the floor and under the house.

"That fitting wasn't on there right, damn it," Steve muttered and dropped through the hole in the floor.

"Should have checked it out with the water on low," Joe pointed out and got a glare from Rafe in response.

"What happened?" Katie asked and both men turned to look at her.

"Nothing huge," Joe assured her. "Just got to tighten things up. Looks worse than it is."

Katie hoped so, because it looked like a lake was in her kitchen and she couldn't think that was a good thing.

Joe slapped one hand on Rafe's shoulder and said, "I should have checked his work personally before we tested it. Rafe's been out of the game for a while, so he may be rusty. But he's got potential."

Katie saw the flicker of annoyance cross Rafe's features and she shared it.

"Isn't Steve the plumber?" she asked pointedly.

"Yeah," Joe said, "but Rafe did the joint work on that pipe."

"It was fine," Rafe said. "That shouldn't have happened."

"Sure, sure," Joe told him, then looked at Katie. "My fault. Like I said, I should have kept a closer eye on the new guy's work."

Rafe was biting his tongue, no doubt worried about defending himself and maybe losing his job. Then she realized that he could be fired anyway, if Joe decided that his work was too sloppy. So before she could stop herself, she stepped in to defend him. "Rafe does excellent work. He set up my temporary kitchen, allowing me to keep my business going. He's stayed late everyday cleaning up and making sure I'm inconvenienced as little as possible. I'm sure that whatever happened with that pipe was unavoidable."

"Yeah," a voice came rumbling up from under the house. "Found the problem. The first joint worked itself loose, so the water had to go somewhere. My bad. I'll get it fixed and we'll be back in business."

Katie gave Joe a look that said quite clearly, *See? You blamed the wrong man.* She smiled at Rafe and left them to clean up the mess and get back to work.

"What was that all about?" Joe wondered.

Steve poked his head up from under the floorboards and smiled widely. "Sounds to me like the boss lady has a thing for Rafe. Lucky bastard."

"Shut up, Steve," Rafe said, but his gaze was locked on the empty doorway where Katie had been standing only a moment before.

Joe was riding him because he could and Rafe would take it because it was all part of the bet he'd lost. Good-natured teasing was all part of working a job. But Katie's defense of him had surprised him. Hell, he couldn't even remember the last time someone had stood up for him—not counting his half-brothers and cousins.

Katie Charles was like no one he'd ever met before. She didn't want anything from him. Wasn't trying to get on his good side. But then, that was because she thought his name was Rafe Cole.

It would be an entirely different story if she knew he was a King.

Three

Rafe was late getting to the job site.

Despite the bet he was in the process of paying off, he had his regular job to do, too. And dealing with a supplier who wasn't coming through for them was one of the tasks he enjoyed most.

"Look Mike," he said, tightening his grip on the phone. "You said we'd have the doors and windows on site at the medical complex by noon yesterday."

"Is it my fault if things got hung up on the East Coast?"

"Probably not," Rafe conceded, "but it's your fault if you don't get this straightened out in the next—" he checked his watch "—five hours."

"That's impossible," the older man on the other end of the line argued.

"All depends on how determined you are, now doesn't it?" Rafe wasn't going to listen to the man's excuses.

This was the second time Mike Prentice had failed to come through for King Construction. It would be the last.

Rafe didn't put up with failure. Mistakes happened to everyone, he knew that. But if a man couldn't keep track of his own business, then he was too disorganized to count on. The Kings required the people they worked with to have the same diligence they showed. "You have the materials at the job site by end of day today."

"Or...?" Mike asked.

A slow smile curved his mouth. Mike couldn't see it, but he must have heard it when Rafe answered, "You really don't want to know, do you?"

"Things happen, Rafe," the man continued to try to defend himself. "I can't stay on top of every supplier I have, you know."

"Don't see why not," Rafe countered. "I do."

"Right. Well, I'm betting that every once in a while someone stiffs the Kings, too."

"Yeah, they do." He glanced around his office at King Construction, already moving on from this particular problem. "But it doesn't happen often and it never repeats itself. This isn't the first time we've had this conversation, Mike. I took your explanation last time, but this is your second chance. I guarantee you, we'll never have this discussion again. If you can't get the supplies to us in five hours, King Construction will find a new supplier for this job."

"Now just wait a minute, let's not be hasty."

"You get *one* second chance with King Construction, Mike," Rafe told him flatly. "And this was it. Now, you have the materials there, as we agreed, or I'll put the word out to every construction outfit in the state that you can't be trusted. How many jobs you think you'll get then?"

A long moment of tense silence passed while the other man did some fast thinking. Rafe knew what was going through the guy's mind. He'd already ruined his rep with the Kings, but he still had hundreds of other construction outfits to do business with. Unless he messed this up further.

"It'll be there," the man said, but he didn't sound happy about it. "You're a hard man, Rafe."

"You should've remembered that, Mike."

Rafe hung up then, leaned back in his desk chair and spun it around until he could look out the window at the ocean scene stretching out in front of him. The King Construction building sat directly on Pacific Coast Highway and each of the brothers had an office with a view. One of the perks of being an owner.

Another perk was reaming guys who failed them.

Standing up, Rafe leaned one hand on the window, feeling the cool of the glass seep into his skin. Was he a hard man? He supposed so.

His ex-wife sure as hell thought so.

Just another reason for him to keep his distance from Katie Charles.

A woman like that didn't need a hard man in her life.

"Now, isn't this a nice view?"

Katie rolled her eyes and laughed at her grandmother. "You're impossible."

Emily O'Hara grinned, fluffed her stylishly trimmed silver hair and then winked at her granddaughter. "Honey, if you don't like looking at handsome men, they might as well bury you."

They were standing at the edge of the yard, watching the action. The men worked together seamlessly, each of them concentrating on a certain area, then helping each other out when needed. Naturally, Nana had noticed Rafe right away, but Katie could hardly blame her. The man was really worth watching.

Katie's gaze went directly to Rafe, on the opposite side of the yard. Since that morning when she'd stood up for him to Joe, Rafe had been avoiding her. She couldn't quite figure out why, either. Maybe it was a guy thing, embarrassing to have a woman defend his honor? She smiled to herself at the thought.

"Well, well. I can see now that you're doing plenty of noticing." She draped one arm around Katie's shoulders. "He's quite the hunk, isn't he?"

"Hunk?" Katie repeated with a laugh.

"You betcha. The question is, what're you going to do about it?"

"What can I do?" Katie watched Rafe as he grinned at something Arturo said and she felt a delicious flutter in the pit of her stomach.

"Honestly," Nana said with a shake of her head, "youth really is wasted on the wrong people. Katie, if you want him, go for it."

"He's not a cookie I can grab and wrap up."

"Who said anything about wrapping him up?" Nana laughed and advised, "I was thinking more that you should *unwrap* him. Just grab him and take a bite. Life's too short, honey. You've got to enjoy it while you can."

"Unbelievably enough," Katie said, "I'm not as freewheeling as my grandmother."

"Well, you could be." Nana shook her head and said, "I loved your grandfather, honey, but he's been gone a long time and I'm still alive and kicking. And, so are *you*. You've been burying yourself in your work for so long, it's a wonder you can step outside without squinting into the sun like a mole."

"I'm not that bad!"

"Didn't used to be," her grandmother allowed. "Until that Cordell twisted you all up."

Katie frowned at the reminder.

"There's a whole wide world full of people out there and half of them are men," Nana told her. "You can't let one bad guy ruin your opinion on an entire gender."

Is that what she was doing? Katie wondered. She didn't think so. Sure, Cordell King had hurt her, but she wasn't hiding. She was working. Building her business. Just because she hadn't been on a date in…good night. She hadn't been on an actual date with an actual man since Cordell and that was more than six months ago now.

How had that happened?

She used to be fun.

She used to call her friends and go out.

She used to have a life.

"Oooh, here comes the cute one," her grandmother whispered.

Katie came out of her thoughts and watched Rafe approaching them. He wasn't cute, she thought. He was dark and dangerous and so sexy just watching him walk made her toes curl. Golden retrievers were cute.

Rafe was…tempting.

"What'd you say his name was?"

"Rafe. Rafe Cole."

"Hmm…"

Katie looked at her grandmother, but the woman's expression was carefully blank. Which usually meant there was something going on in Nana's mind that she didn't want anyone else to know about. But before Katie could wriggle the information out of her, Rafe was standing in front of them. She made the introductions, then Rafe spoke up.

"I just wanted to tell you that we'll be shutting down early tonight. Joe's got a meeting and he wants Arturo and Steve there."

"Not you?" she asked.

He shook his head. "No reason for me to be there. I'm just a worker bee. Anyway," he said, with a smile for her grandmother, "it was nice to meet you."

"Good to meet you too, Rafe," Nana said with a smile.

When he walked away, Katie's gaze was locked on him. His long legs, the easy, confident strides he took, the way the sunlight glinted on his black hair. And yes, she admitted silently, she liked the view of his butt in those faded jeans, too.

Finally though, she turned her gaze to her grandmother. The thoughtful expression on her Nana's face had her asking, "Okay, what's going on? What're you thinking?"

"Me? Only wondering if he has a grandfather as good looking as he is."

"You're hiding something," Katie said, narrowing her eyes.

"Me?" Emily slapped one hand to her chest and widened her eyes in innocence. "I'm an open book, sweetie. What you see is what you get."

"Nana…"

She checked her wristwatch and said, "Oh, I have to fly. Grace and I have a double date tonight with a couple of frisky widowers. I'm meeting Grace for manicures in half an hour."

Katie laughed and gave her a hug. "You're amazing."

"So are you, when you give yourself a chance." Emily slid a look at Rafe again. "Why not invite that boy to dinner? Live a little, Katie. You like him, don't you?"

"Yeah," Katie said, shifting her gaze back to Rafe. "I do. I mean, I've only known him a week, but I've spent so much time with him, it feels like longer. He's a nice guy, Nana. A regular guy. Nothing like Cordell King and believe me, that's a good thing. I've had it with the idle rich."

"Not all rich guys are idle," Emily pointed out. "Or, jerks for that matter."

"Maybe," Katie said, but she wasn't convinced. Granted, she hadn't had a lot of experience with rich men. Cordell had been the one and only billionaire she'd ever known. But if he was an example of their breed, then he was more than enough to last her a lifetime. "From now on though, I'm only interested in regular, hardworking guys."

"You have your mother's hard head, God bless her." Nana blew out a breath and said, "Fine. This Rafe seems nice enough and he's surely easy on the eyes."

"That he is," Katie agreed, letting her gaze slide back to the man whose image had been filling her dreams lately.

"But you never really know a man until you've hit the sack with him."

"Nana!" Katie groaned and shook her head. "What kind of role model are you, anyway?"

"The good kind." Emily laughed, clearly delighted at being able to shock her granddaughter so easily. "I'm just saying, it might be interesting to take him out for a test drive, that's all."

Katie loved her grandmother, but she was in no way the free spirit Emily O'Hara was. But then Nana hadn't always been this outspoken and full of adventure. Right after Katie's mother died, Nana had seemed to realize just how short life really was and she'd thrown herself into the mix with abandon.

And while Katie admired that adventurous style and certainly understood, she just couldn't bring herself to behave the same way. Nana had had the great love of her life and now she was looking for fun.

Katie was still looking for love.

Still, the fact was, Nana was probably right about Rafe. Katie was more drawn to him than she had been to anyone, up to and including Cordell King. So maybe it was time she took a chance. Pushed herself out of the cocoon she'd wrapped herself in.

"Not interested in a test drive." Okay, that's a lie, she amended silently when that little buzz of interest popped in her veins again. "Not yet, anyway," she said aloud. "But dinner would be good. I do like him and he's so different from Cordell King."

"Uh-huh."

"What?"

"Nothing. Not a darn thing." Emily pulled her in for a hard, tight hug and said, "I'm off for some fun. I suggest you do the same. Gotta run."

Alone again, Katie silently studied Rafe Cole as he stood in the sunlight laughing with Arturo.

Fun sounded like a good idea.

"The guys are gone," Rafe said.

He had stayed deliberately, after the crew left for the

night, just to get a few minutes alone with her. Hadn't asked himself why, because he wasn't sure he'd like the answer. But he'd fallen into the habit of being the last man to leave and he actually looked forward to the times when it was just him and Katie at the house.

The neighborhood was quiet, but for the muffled, heartbeat-like sound of a basketball thumping in someone's driveway. A dog barked from close by and the ocean wind felt cool after a long day in the sun.

Katie had her curly red hair pulled back in a ponytail and her green eyes were shining in the afternoon light. A soft smile curved her mouth and Rafe felt a punch of need slam into him. He knew it would be a mistake to get her into bed. After all, not only was she so not his type, but she hated the King family. If they had sex and she found out he'd lied about who he was, it could only get ugly.

But damned if logic had anything to do with what he was feeling at the moment.

"How'd it go today?" She stepped out of the house and started for the garage. Rafe walked with her.

"We got the drywall up over the pipes and the plumbing's finished."

"Really?" She stopped and grinned. "No more naked pipes!"

The smile on her face made her eyes shine brighter and Rafe felt a tug of something hot and wicked. The woman could turn him hard without even trying. He couldn't even remember a time when he'd been this attracted, this quickly to anyone. Not even Leslie, the ex-wife from hell, had had this effect on him.

After a moment or two, he cleared his throat and said, "Yeah. It should move pretty quickly now, as long as all of your supplies come in on time."

She held up both hands, fingers crossed, and said, "Here's hoping. I really miss having a kitchen."

"Maybe, but from the smells coming from your temporary setup, it's not slowing you down any."

Laughing, she opened the garage door and stepped into the gloom. Rafe stayed with her, not ready to leave yet. He took a quick look around the garage. It was tidy, like the rest of her house. Storage shelves on one wall, washer and drier on another. There was an older model, red SUV parked dead center and a few lawn and garden tools stacked along the last wall.

"Baking the cookies is easy enough thanks to you setting up the stove for me," she said, with a nod of her head. "But oh, I miss my counter when it comes time to decorate and wrap. I've got tables set up all over the patio now, but…"

"You want your life back," he finished for her.

"Yes," she agreed with a sigh. "Funny, but you go along every day and you hardly notice your routine—" She paused and smiled. "You'll notice I said routine, not *rut*."

"I noticed," he said with a grin.

She stopped beside the shelves and bent down to pull a bag of charcoal free. He bent down at the same time and suddenly, their mouths were just a kiss apart. Time staggered to a standstill. His gaze dropped to her lips and everything inside him clenched when her tongue slipped out to slide along her bottom lip.

Rafe wanted a taste of her. More than he did his next breath. But her eyes told him she wasn't ready for that and if there was one thing Rafe King knew, it was how to be patient. So he straightened up and grabbed the bag.

"Let me get that for you."

She stepped back with a soft *thanks,* then continued with what she'd been saying. "Then you get ripped out of that routine and all you can think about is getting it back. That doesn't make any sense at all, does it?"

"Sure it does," he said, idly noting how the sunlight drifting in through the small garage windows shone on her hair like fire. His body was tight and his breath was strangling in his lungs. But he didn't let her know that.

"Nobody likes having their place invaded and their life turned upside down."

"What about you?" she asked. "Do you have a routine you don't want upset?"

He gave her a quick grin and set the bag of charcoal at his feet. "Men don't have routines," he corrected. "We have schedules."

"Ah." She leaned against the front fender of the van. "And your 'schedule'?"

"Same as everyone else's I guess," he said after a long minute, when he took the time to remind himself to be vague. He couldn't exactly tell her about time spent with his brothers, or at King Construction. "Work, home. Play."

"I know what you do for work. What's your idea of playtime?"

"Well now," he mused thoughtfully, meeting her gaze and allowing her to see exactly what she was doing to him, "that's an interesting question."

She sucked in a breath of air and straightened up and away from her car. He liked seeing her nervous. That told him she was feeling the same kind of attraction he was. Good to know. But he'd let her catch her breath before he pushed any harder. He wasn't used to dealing with a woman like Katie.

The women he generally spent time with were, like Rafe, only interested in a few hours of pleasure. There were no hidden agendas, no emotional traps and no expectations. Katie was different. She was new territory for him and damned if he wasn't enjoying himself.

"So?" he asked, picking up the bag of charcoal, "Barbecuing?"

She looked grateful for the reprieve. "Yes. Hamburgers sounded good to me and they're just not the same if they're not barbecued."

"Agreed," Rafe said, turning for the door. "Want me to set it up for you?"

"Only if you'll stay for dinner."

He stopped, half turned and looked at her. A slow smile curved his mouth. If he was here for dinner, he'd be damn sure staying for dessert, too. "That'd be great. But if it's all the same to you, I'll go home and shower and change first."

"Sure, that's fine."

She looked nervous again, chewing at her bottom lip. His gaze locked on that action and his insides tightened even further. Oh, yeah. He'd make it a cold shower, too.

"Okay," he said, "give me an hour? I'll get the barbecue going when I get back. I'm good at starting fires."

"That," she said, "I absolutely believe."

Four

"It doesn't mean a thing," Katie told herself while she quickly mixed up a batch of pasta salad to go with the burgers. "It's just dinner. A barbecue. Friendly. Non-threatening. Not sexual in any way…"

Oh, even *she* didn't believe that. She'd felt the tension mounting between them when they both went to reach for the bag of charcoal. For a second, she had been sure he was going to kiss her and she still wasn't sure if she'd been relieved or disappointed that he hadn't. And, she had seen his eyes when he promised to start her fire for her. He probably knew that he'd already started it.

Cooking helped center her. It always had. As a girl, she'd helped Nana out in the kitchen and slowly learned her way around a recipe. Then, she started creating her own. And she had learned early that no matter what else was happening in her life, the kitchen was her comfort zone.

She chopped celery, then mushrooms, carrots and broccoli, and added them to the cold pasta, giving it all a good stir together with the homemade pesto. When she was finished, she stored the bowl in her fridge and started on dessert.

She had to keep busy. If she stopped long enough to think about what she was doing, she'd talk herself out of it.

That brought her up short.

"Out of *what* exactly, Katie?" she demanded. "He's coming for dinner. Nobody said anything about sex."

Oh, boy.

The problem was, she really wanted Rafe Cole. She'd been around him almost nonstop for the last week and every day, he'd gotten to her just a little bit more. He was friendly and helpful and, boy, he looked darn good in his jeans. Those blue eyes of his were starring nightly in her dreams and her fingers itched to slide through his thick, black hair.

Yep, she was in bad shape and no doubt asking for trouble by instigating this dinner. But maybe it was time she had a little trouble in her life. She'd always been the good girl. Always done the "right" thing. The *safe* thing.

Heck, she'd dated Cordell King for three months and hadn't slept with him. She'd wanted to take it slow because she'd been so sure that he was the one.

It had seemed, at the time, as if fate had thrown them together. After all, it wasn't as if she stumbled across billionaires all the time in her everyday life. He had ordered an extra-large cookie bouquet to be delivered to his assistant, who was taking off for maternity leave. Katie's delivery girl hadn't been able to take the runs that day, so Katie had done the job herself.

Cordell had slipped out of his office to watch as his assistant cooed and cried over the beautifully frosted cookies that Katie presented to her. And after that, he'd walked Katie to her car and asked her to dinner. After that night, they'd been together as often as each of their schedules had allowed.

Looking back, Katie could see that she had been flattered by Cordell's attention. That the thought of a rich, successful man being interested in her had fed the flames of what she had believed was the start of something amazing. He was so handsome. So attentive. So damned sexy. Her heart had taken a leap before her mind could catch up.

Shaking her head, she realized that she had felt at the time as if she were living in a fairy tale. Where the handsome prince swooped into her poor but proud cottage and carried her off to her castle.

"Silly," she whispered, thinking back to her own actions. Thank God she hadn't slept with him. That would have only fed the humiliation when she looked back on a time where she had been involved in what she thought was something special.

As it turned out, of course, the only thing special they shared was that they were both in love with Cordell.

Grumbling under her breath, Katie let the old, hurtful memories fade away as she focused instead on the evening to come. She spooned fresh whipped cream into old-fashioned sundae glasses. Then she layered chocolate-chip cookie bits with more whipped cream and when they were finished, they too went into the fridge. She would drizzle raspberry syrup over the top of the frothy dessert just before she served it.

When the meal was done, she glanced around the temporary kitchen, checked her watch and realized that

Rafe would be arriving any minute. So she raced to the bathroom and checked her hair and makeup. Stupid, but she felt like a teenager waiting for her first date to arrive.

Nerves bubbled in the pit of her stomach and a kind of excitement she hadn't felt before hummed through her bloodstream. Staring at the woman in the mirror, she gave herself a little pep talk.

"You're going to have fun, Katie Charles. For once in your life, you're not going to think ahead to tomorrow. You're going to enjoy tonight for whatever it turns out to be." She nodded abruptly and pretended she didn't see the flash of nervousness staring back at her from her own eyes. "He's a nice guy. You're both single. So relax, already."

Easier said than done, she knew.

But there was nothing wrong with a little fun.

Right?

"You find out anything from the family?" Rafe asked his brother as he steered his truck down Katie's street.

"Not a damn thing," Sean assured him, his voice crackling with static over the cell phone. "I talked to Tanner, but since he and Ivy got married, he's pretty much useless for picking up stray news. All he talks about is their latest ultrasound picture." Sean sighed in disgust. "Seriously, you'd think they were the only people in the universe to get pregnant."

Rafe let that one go. He was glad for their brother Tanner. Ivy was a nice woman and against all odds, she was turning Tanner into a halfway decent Christmas-tree farmer.

"Then," Sean said, "I called cousin Jesse. But the only thing he knows about Katie Charles is that he favors her macadamia-nut-white-chocolate-chip cookies. His wife Bella says the peanut-butter ones are best, but their boy Joshua likes the chocolate fudge."

Rafe rubbed a spot between his eyes and took a breath. "And I care what kind of cookies they like, because…"

"Because that's the only information they had and now I want a damn cookie," Sean grumbled.

Rafe scowled as he pulled up outside Katie's house. He parked and slanted a glance at the setting sun reflecting off the gleaming front windows. "Somebody in the family knows her and I want to find out who."

"What do you care?" Sean snorted a laugh. "I mean, seriously dude, you've known her for what, a week? What's it to you if she hates the Kings?"

"I don't like it."

"You'd think you'd be used to it," Sean said. "There are plenty of people out there who feel the same."

"Not *women.*"

"Good point." Sean sighed and said, "So, this is part of why you find her so interesting, huh?"

"Maybe." He didn't even know. But Katie Charles was hitting him in places he hadn't known existed. And she kept doing it. One look out of those green eyes of hers and his mind filled with all sorts of damn near irresistible images.

And it was lowering to admit that if she knew he was a King, she'd slam her front door in his face and he'd never see her again.

"Fine. I'll go back to the drawing board. Hey, I'll call Garrett," Sean suggested. "He loves a mystery, so if he doesn't have the answer he'll find it."

Sean was right. Their cousin, Garrett King, ran a security company and liked nothing better than delving for secrets. If anyone could find out who was behind Katie's feelings about the Kings, it would be Garrett.

"All right, good. Thanks."

"You busy? I'm taking the jet to Vegas tonight. Why don't you come with me? We'll hit a show, then wipe out the craps tables."

Rafe smiled. Ordinarily, he'd have appreciated the invitation. But tonight, he had something better to do. "Thanks, but I've got plans."

"With the King hater?"

"Her name is Katie, but yeah," Rafe said tightly.

"She doesn't know who you are, does she?"

"No." Irritation hummed inside him again. He'd never before had to disguise himself to be with a woman. Hell, if anything, the King name had women clamoring to get near him.

"Great. Well, pick me up some cookies before she finds out you're lying to her and you ruin what's left of our rep with her."

Rafe hung up a second or two later, his brother's words ringing in his ears. He dismissed them though, because there was no way Katie would find out Rafe's last name until he was good and ready for her to know. And that wouldn't be until he'd romanced her, seduced her and shown her just how likeable he really was.

Then he'd tell her he was a King. And she'd see how wrong she was. About all of them.

But for now, he was enjoying himself with a woman who didn't want anything from him beyond barbecuing some burgers.

He got out of the truck and headed for the house. But before he reached the porch, Katie rushed out the door and skidded to a stop when she saw him. Her curly red hair was loose around her shoulders and her long legs looked tan and gorgeous in a pair of white shorts. Her dark green T-shirt made her eyes shine as she spotted him. "Rafe, I'm so glad you're back! Follow me!"

She sprinted down her front steps and past him, headed toward her neighbor's house. She rounded a white picket fence with bright splashes of flowers climbing across it and headed up the driveway. Rafe stayed right on her heels, his mind already racing to possible disasters. Someone dying. Someone bleeding. He reached into his pocket and gripped his phone ready to dial nine-one-one.

Adrenaline pulsed through him as they rushed up the drive to the front porch of a small, Tudor-style cottage with a sloping roof and leaded windows.

"What's wrong?" he shouted.

"Nicole needs help!"

The front door of the house swung open as they approached and a harried woman with short, blond hair and a toddler on her hip sighed in relief.

"Thank God you're here, it's all over everywhere."

Katie made to run inside, but Rafe pulled her back and went in first. He didn't know what the hell was going on around here, but damned if he was going to let Katie run into the heart of whatever trouble it was.

She was right behind him though. He took a moment to glance around, while looking for whatever disaster had happened. He registered the toy cars strewn across the floor and the wooden train set. Then he heard the trouble and his heartbeat returned to normal. No one was dying but it sounded like there was an indoor fountain on full blast.

The woman was talking to Katie, but Rafe was only half listening.

"I can't turn the water off—it's like the valve is frozen

in place or something and there's water everywhere and Connor was crying.…"

"It's okay, Nicole," Katie said. "We'll get it shut off and help you clean it up."

He ignored the women and headed for the kitchen, following the loud sound of splashing. Not the way Rafe had planned on this first date with Katie going, but he could adapt. Water was shooting out from under the kitchen sink through the open cupboard doors. Already there was a small flood in the room and a kitchen rug was drifting out on the tide.

Cursing under his breath, Rafe sloshed his way through the kitchen. He crouched down in front of the sink, reached through the cascading cold water and blindly found the shutoff valve. Water poured over him in a never-ending jet. He blinked it out of his eyes, muttered an oath and grabbed hold of the damn valve. Hell, he thought, no wonder Nicole hadn't been able to turn it. It took everything he had to budge the damn thing and it didn't go easy, fighting him every inch of the way. By increments, he slowly shut down the torrent until all that was left was the mess on the floor and a steady drip under the sink.

The sudden silence was almost overpowering. Until the little boy in his mother's arms started laughing.

"Boat!" he cried, pointing to a cell phone as it floated past them.

"Fabulous," Nicole murmured and bent down to scoop it up. "Well, I needed an upgrade anyway."

"Oh, honey, I'm so sorry," Katie said, dropping one arm around her friend's shoulders. She looked at Rafe, soaking wet, and winced. "Rafe Cole, this is Nicole Baxter. Nicole, Rafe."

The woman gave him a tired smile. "I suspect I'm happier to meet you than you are me at the moment."

"No problem. I like an adventure every now and then." He pushed his hair back from his face with both hands, then swept water off his palms. Wet and cold, he caught the glimmer of regret and amusement in Katie's eyes and smiled in spite of everything. "I've got it shut off, but your pipe joint's shot. It has to be fixed."

"Of course it does," Nicole said with a sigh. She hitched her son a little higher on her hip and added, "Thanks. Really, for shutting off Old Faithful. I never would have been able to do it."

"Your husband should be able to replace it without a problem," he told her.

"My *ex*-husband's in Hawaii with his secretary," she said wryly and only then did Rafe see Katie shaking her head at him in a silent signal to shut up.

"Haven't seen him since before Connor was born," Nicole added, kissing the little guy's cheek. "But we do fine, don't we, sweet boy?"

Perfect, Rafe thought. He'd made the woman feel even worse now by reminding her of her creep of an ex. A bubble of irritation frothed inside him. What kind of man walked away from his child? Rafe didn't get it. Sure, he knew that marriages didn't always work out. But what man would walk away from his own baby? Shouldn't he try to hold his family together?

While his brain raced, a quiet, rational voice in the back of his mind warned him that he was putting his own issues out there and it was time to draw them back. His old man hadn't been even close to a normal father, but at least Ben King was always there when his kids needed him. Which was more than Rafe could say for Nicole's ex.

Still, looking at Katie's friend, holding her son so closely, reminded him of his own upbringing. Oh, his mother hadn't stuck around or anything. She'd handed him off to an elderly aunt before he was a year old and only showed up for a visit when her money was running out. Ben King hadn't married her, but he'd supported her until Rafe was eighteen.

Once he was grown, his mom had started coming to Rafe for the cash she required to live the kind of life she preferred. He didn't mind paying. It kept her out of his hair.

Now though, watching Nicole and her son brought home to him again how hard the aunt who'd raised him had had it. Oh, she'd had money for plumbing repairs, but she'd been all alone raising a boy. Just as Nicole was. And Nicole didn't have the luxury of calling a King for help.

Lucky for her, there was already a King in the neighborhood.

He looked at Katie and saw the worry for her friend shining in her eyes and he heard himself say, "Why don't you two get the back door open and sweep out as much of this water as you can?"

"Good idea," Katie agreed. "Come on, Nicole, I'll help you get this straightened up."

"You don't have to do that," the blond said. "We'll be fine. Really."

"Sure you will, I can see that," Rafe told her with a shrug, not wanting to wound her pride. "But while you two get the water out of here, I'm going to run up to the hardware store. I'll get a new joint in there and have you up and running again."

Katie *beamed* at him.

And he felt as if someone had just pinned a medal to his chest.

Their gazes locked, and the rest of the world fell away for one long, sizzling moment. Every heartbeat felt measured. Every breath a struggle.

Rafe was caught by the emotion on her face. The pride in *him*. The gratitude and the admiration. He had never known another moment like it. It was amazing, he thought, to have someone look at him as if he'd hung the moon.

And all he wanted to do was walk across the floor, take her into his arms and sweep her into a dip for a kiss that would send them both over the edge of hunger. Need was a gnawing ache inside him. He'd never experienced *that* before, either, he thought. Desire, sure. Want, absolutely.

But *need?*

Never.

"I can't ask you to do that," Nicole said, shattering the moment.

Rafe took a breath to steady himself and shook his head, clearing his thoughts, getting a grip on the emotions suddenly churning through him. As he regained control, he mentally thanked Nicole for shattering whatever it was that had so briefly hummed between he and Katie.

Looking at the blonde, he said, "You didn't ask. I offered. And don't worry about it. Besides," he added with a grin for the toddler, "with this little guy around, you're going to need water, right?"

Katie was still smiling at him as if he were some kind of comic-book hero. And she was still stirring him up inside, so he gave her a smile, then tugged his keys out of his jeans pocket. Best all around if he left now. "I'll be back in a few minutes and we'll get you set up."

"Thanks." Nicole whispered the word. "Really."

Katie gave her a brief hug, then stepped up to Rafe and slid her hand into his. "I'll walk you to the door while Nicole gets the broom and mop."

His fingers curled around hers and he felt the heat of her skin zing through his system like a raging wildfire. At the front door, Katie looked back over her shoulder to make sure Nicole was out of earshot, then said softly, "Thank you for offering to help her like that, Rafe. Nicole couldn't afford a plumber. You're really doing something amazing for her."

"It's not a problem."

"For *you*," she said with another smile. "But for a single mom, it's a catastrophe. Or it would have been. Without you. You're my hero."

Her simple words hit him with a crash. Always before, when people needed help, he wrote a check. Made a donation. It was safe, distant and still managed to salve the urge he had to help those who needed it. He hadn't realized until just now how differently helping felt when it was up close and personal.

"I've never been anybody's hero before."

She looked up at him and he knew he could lose himself in the deep, summer green of her eyes. Her delectable mouth curved at the edges. "You are now."

He reached up and cupped the back of her neck with his palm. "Keep that thought and hold on to it for later, okay?"

"I can do that," she said and went up on her toes to brush a soft kiss across his mouth. Then she stepped away and said, "Hurry back."

His lips were tingling, his breath was still strangling

in his lungs and Rafe was suddenly so damn hard he didn't think he'd be able to walk to his truck without limping.

Some hero.

Nicole and Connor joined them for the barbecue.

Katie told herself she was just being nice—Nicole was still upset and they were all tired out from cleaning up the mess in her kitchen. But the truth was, that moment with Rafe at the front door of Nicole's house had shaken Katie enough that she had wanted someone else around during dinner. Not exactly a chaperone, just someone to keep Katie from jumping Rafe the moment they were alone.

Because that's exactly what she wanted to do. He had been wonderful. Honestly, she thought back to her time with Cordell King and no matter how she tried to imagine it, she couldn't see that man diving under a kitchen sink to fix something as a favor. He was too much a suit-and-tie man. Too focused on the bottom line of his company and not so interested in the "real world."

Rafe though, was different, she thought, watching him gently toss a soft foam ball to Connor. The little boy waved both arms trying to catch it and Rafe laughed with him when he missed. The man was just...

"Amazing," Nicole said, unknowingly finishing Katie's mental sentence.

"What?"

"Him." Nicole smiled at Katie, then shifted her gaze to where her son was playing with Rafe. "That guy is one in a million, Katie."

"I was just thinking the same thing."

"Yeah?" Nicole pushed her paper plate aside, leaned

both arms on the weathered picnic table and asked, "If you think so, why'd you have Connor and I come over and horn in on your date?"

"You're not horning in," Katie argued. In the year she and her son had lived next door, Nicole had become Katie's best friend. They'd commiserated on the rotten tendencies of the men they'd had in their lives and they'd bonded over working from home. Katie had her cookie company and Nicole did the billing for several local companies.

"You're my friend, Nicole, and you're always invited over. You know that."

"'Course I know that." Nicole reached out and covered Katie's hand with her own. "You've been great to us since we moved in here. But Katie, this is the first guy I've seen you date in like forever. Don't you want some alone time?"

Katie stared at Rafe as he scooped Connor up and ran across the yard, the little boy chortling happily. "I do and I don't. Seriously, Nicole, I'm not sure what I want."

"Well I can tell you if he looked at *me,* the way he looks at *you,* I wouldn't have any trouble deciding what I wanted."

"It's complicated."

"I know. Cordell." Giving her hand a squeeze, Nicole sat back and shook her head. "He messed you up bad. But Rafe isn't Cordell."

"You're telling me," Katie said on a sigh.

"Do you really want to risk losing a great guy because you're still mad at a rotten one?"

"Have you been talking to Nana?"

Nicole laughed. "No. I haven't. But if she agrees with

me, then we're both right and you should trust us on this. Give it a shot, Katie. What've you got to lose?"

Another chunk of her heart, she thought but didn't say. But then again, if she never risked her heart, she'd never use it, would she? She'd die an old lady, filled with regrets, still holding on to her withered pride like a trophy with some of the shiny worn off.

Her gaze locked on Rafe again as he lifted the little boy high enough for tiny hands to swat at the glossy leaves of an orange tree. Her still-wary heart turned over in her chest as she watched the expression on Rafe's face. He was enjoying himself. He was relaxed, at ease with her friends, in her tiny backyard. Cordell, in the same situation, would have—never mind, he never would have been in this situation. He had preferred five-star restaurants to picnics and three-piece suits to jeans.

Cordell had swept Katie off her feet because she had never been with anyone like him. Now she knew she should have kept it that way.

But Rafe...he was different from Cordell. He was the kind of guy Katie should have met first.

And if she had, she asked herself, would she have been so hesitant to take a chance on him? No, she wouldn't have.

"Ooh, I can see by the look in your eyes you've decided to take a chance," Nicole said. "Want me to take Connor home so you can get going on that?"

Katie shook her head. "Not until after dessert," she said. "Then we'll see what happens."

She stood up and headed for the enclosed patio and her refrigerator. Behind her, she heard Connor's giggles and Rafe's deep laughter.

Her skin tingled and everything in her awoke to anticipation.

Five

"If that dessert was a sample of your cookies," Rafe said much later, "then I can understand why people are so crazy about them."

"Thank you. I can give you some to take home if you like," Katie said.

Rafe tipped his head to one side and studied her. Nicole and her son had gone home and now it was just he and Katie in the backyard. The summer night was cool, the sky overhead swimming with stars. Moonlight drifted down and did battle with the candle flames flickering in the soft breeze.

"Anxious to get rid of me?" he asked quietly.

"No," she said. "That's not what I meant. I just—oh, for heaven's sake. You'd think I'd never been on a date before." She caught herself and amended, "Not that this is a date or anything…"

Rafe grinned, enjoying that touch of nervousness. "It's not?"

"Is it?"

His smile firmly in place he admitted, "Well, I don't usually do plumbing on a date, but everything else seems about right."

Now she returned his smile and seemed to relax a little. The wind lifted her hair like a lover's caress. "It was fun, wasn't it?"

"Yeah, and it's not over yet."

"Really."

Not a question, he told himself. More of a challenge. Well, he was willing to accept it. "Really."

He stood up, walked to her side of the picnic table and pulled her to her feet. "What're you doing?"

"I want to dance with you," he said simply, drawing her closer.

Even as she went with him, she was saying, "There's no music."

"Sure there is," he told her, wrapping his arm around her waist and capturing her right hand in his left. "You're just not listening hard enough."

She shook her head at him.

"Close your eyes," he said and she did. He looked down at her, so trusting, so beautiful, and his breath caught in his chest. Her hand was warm and smooth in his, her scent—a mixture of vanilla and cinnamon—filling him. He smiled, thinking that she smelled as edible as her cookies.

"Now listen," he urged quietly, his voice hardly more than a whisper of sound.

"To what?" she answered just as quietly.

"Everything."

He swayed with her in his arms and rested his chin

on top of her head. Her body felt perfect aligned along his and he went hard and ready almost instantly. If she noticed, she didn't let him know.

As they moved in the starlight, sounds of the summer night began to encroach. Crickets singing, the distant sigh of the ocean, the wind in the trees. It was as if nature herself were providing a perfect symphony just for the two of them.

She smiled, tipped her head back, and keeping her eyes closed, moved with him as if they'd been dancing together forever. "I hear it now," she whispered. "It's perfect."

"Yeah," he said, coming to a stop, staring down at her. "It is."

Her eyes opened and she met his gaze. "Rafe?"

His hand tightened on hers and he held her closer, pulling her in firmly enough against him that she couldn't miss feeling exactly what she was doing to him. "I want you, Katie. More than I've ever wanted anything."

A tiny sigh slipped from her mouth as she confessed, "I feel exactly the same way."

He gave her a grin and slowly lowered his mouth to hers. "Good to hear."

He kissed her and the instant their mouths met, Rafe felt a punch of desire so hot, so unbelievably strong that it nearly knocked him over. In response, his arms tightened around her, all thoughts of dancing disappearing from his mind. He wanted to move with her, but dancing had nothing to do with the plans quickly forming in his mind. He needed her, more than he would have thought possible. And he wanted her even more.

His hands swept up and down her spine, defining

every curve, every valley she possessed. She moved against him, her body restless, her soft moans telling him everything he needed to know. He slipped one hand beneath the hem of her T-shirt and swept up, to caress the side of her breast. Even the lacy material of her bra couldn't keep him from enjoying the heat of her. The perfectly shaped wonder of her. His hands itched to feel her skin.

Hunger roared through him and he deepened their kiss, his tongue sweeping into her mouth, claiming everything she had and silently demanding more. She gave it to him, surrendering herself to the passion rising between them. Her tongue tangled with his, her breath sighing against his cheek as she met him stroke for stroke. Her hands clutched his shoulders, holding on tightly as she moaned in appreciation.

That soft sound was enough to push Rafe dangerously close to the edge. He tore his mouth from hers, looked down at her through eyes glazed with heat and need and said grimly, "If we don't stop right now, I'm going to throw you down onto this picnic table and give your neighbors a show."

A choked laugh shot from her throat. She didn't release her hold on him though, as if she didn't quite trust herself to be able to stand on her own two feet.

"The picnic table's not nearly as comfortable as my bed," she said, just a little breathlessly.

"Is that an invitation?"

"Sounded like one to me."

"All I need to know," Rafe muttered and swept her up into his arms.

"You don't have to carry me!"

"Faster this way," he told her, nearly sprinting across the yard toward the house.

"That works too," she said, snuggling close to him, stroking the flat of her hand across his chest.

He hissed in a breath, hit the patio door and stepped inside. "Where to?"

"Down the hall, turn left at the end."

He was already moving. His body was hard and aching. He could hardly draw a breath without fanning the flames licking at his insides. His heart pounding, Rafe entered her room and strode straight to the bed. Absently, he noticed the window seat on the front wall, colorful rugs scattered across a gleaming wood floor and a squat bookcase stuffed with paperbacks.

But his gaze was locked on the wide bed covered in an old-fashioned quilt. He stopped alongside the four-poster, tossed the covers back to reveal smooth white sheets and dropped Katie onto the mattress.

She bounced, then smiled up at him. It was all the encouragement he needed. Tearing off his clothes, he watched her as she did the same. In seconds, they were both naked and he was leaning over her. Rafe had been thinking about this moment for days. Dreaming about it every damn night.

She was haunting him, this woman who so hated the King family. She had somehow reached him in a way no other woman had and though that admission bothered him, it wasn't enough to keep him from enjoying what she was offering.

Reaching up to him, she plunged her fingers through his hair and drew his mouth down to hers. Their mouths melded and her taste was as intoxicating as ever. Her kiss sizzled inside him, making the ache in his body almost overpowering. Everything in him urged him to hurry. To take. To ease the need clamoring within him.

But the urge to savor was just as strong. His tongue

entwined with hers, he slid one hand down the length of her body, relishing the glide of her skin beneath his palm. So soft, so curvy. So just right.

Reluctantly, he broke their kiss, shifted position slightly and took one of her hard, pink nipples into his mouth. She gasped and arched against him as he suckled her, using his teeth and tongue to lovingly torture her. He felt every breath she took, heard every sigh and wanted more. Rafe inhaled her scent and lost himself in the glory of her.

She held his head to her breast as if afraid he might stop. But Rafe was just getting started. He moved to give the same attention to her other breast, feeling her heartbeat quicken, as anticipation rolled through her. He smiled against her skin, then lifted his head and looked up into her passion glazed eyes. "I've wanted this since the first moment I saw you."

"Me, too," she admitted, licking her bottom lip in an action that caused everything inside him to clench.

His fingers and thumb continued to tug and pull at her nipple, making her squirm and her breath catch in her throat. When he touched her, he saw exactly what she was feeling on her face. He loved watching her expression shift and change as she gave herself over to him and Rafe knew there was something more here than want.

Something dangerous.

Yet he couldn't have pulled away and left if it had meant his life.

That thought stark in his mind, he leaned over her again, stared down into her green eyes and asked, "What are you doing to me?"

She laughed a little and cupped his cheek in her palm. "At the moment, it's *you* doing something to *me*."

Staring into her eyes, he felt that kick of something he didn't quite recognize and after a long second or two, he let it go. Now was not the time to be thinking.

"So it is," he agreed, dipping his head for one brief, hard kiss. He felt it again. That something *more* between them. That extra jolt he'd never known before. A part of Rafe worried that he might be getting in deeper here than he had planned. But there was no way out now. No other answer but to have her. To feel her body welcoming his. To delve into her heat and take them both where they had been heading from the first.

He'd worry about consequences later. Wonder if this had been a good idea another time. For right now, there was nowhere he'd rather be.

Sliding one hand down the length of her body, he stroked her core with the tips of his fingers until she lifted her hips into his touch. Her gaze never left his. He watched passion flare and sparkle in her eyes and pushed her higher, faster. Her breath came in quick gasps. Her body trembled in his arms and he felt her pleasure as if it were his own.

Rafe couldn't get enough of looking at her face. Every emotion so openly displayed. Nothing hidden. Nothing held back. He'd never been with a woman so honestly enthusiastic. Always before, the women in his life had been controlled. As if playing the role they thought he wanted from them.

Even his ex-wife Leslie had held something back from him, as if she couldn't quite trust him enough to confide her deepest feelings and reactions. But there was no artifice with Katie.

She threw herself into the moment and in so doing, drew him with her.

"Come for me," he whispered, dipping his head

to taste her mouth. He caught her breath as it passed between her parted lips. She tasted as sweet as the cookies she was known for. "Let go, Katie. Fly."

She choked off a half laugh and held on to him, one arm draped around his shoulder. Her hips rocked into his hand and when he dipped his fingers in and out of her heat, she groaned and arched high off the bed. "Rafe…"

"Shatter, Katie. Let me watch you shatter."

Her gaze locked on his, she expelled a breath, took another and did as he asked. Her body shook as she cried out his name, her gaze never leaving his. She allowed him to see exactly what he was doing to her. What he was making her feel. And his own passion exploded in response. She bit down hard on her bottom lip and rode the wave of completion he gave her and all Rafe could think was, it wasn't enough. He had to see her face etched in pleasure again and again.

The last of her tremors had barely faded away when he pushed off the bed, grabbed his jeans off the floor and dug into the pocket.

"What're you…" She stopped and smiled when she saw him pull out a foil-wrapped condom. Stretching her arms back over her head, she sighed and said, "Pretty sure of yourself tonight then, weren't you? You came prepared."

He ripped open the foil, sheathed himself and turned back to her. "Not sure of myself. Just hopeful."

He leaned over her and Katie's arms encircled his neck. "I think, Rafe Cole, that you're *always* sure of yourself and tonight was no different."

Couldn't really argue with that, he thought. But the truth was, he had just wanted to be prepared. Unlike his father, Rafe didn't run around the world leaving illegitimate children in his wake. In fact, he had no intention of ever having children and he for damn sure wouldn't create a life because he was too lazy or too selfish to wear a condom.

None of which Katie needed to know.

Bending his head to claim another hard, fast kiss, Rafe looked into her eyes and said, "I'm not so sure of myself around you, Katie. And that's the truth."

She smiled, a slow curve of her mouth, then reached up to stroke her fingertips along his jawline. "I like hearing that."

Wryly, he said, "Thought you would. Women love to know when they've got a man dazed and confused."

"Are you dazed?" she asked, moving against him.

"With any luck," he told her, "I'm about to be."

He parted her thighs and settled himself between them. He looked his fill of her then, stroking her center with long, leisurely caresses until she was writhing with the tension.

"Yeah," he whispered, more to himself than to her, "dazed, all right."

Outside, the night was cool and quiet. In this room, the only sound was their ragged breathing and the thundering beat of their hearts. All that existed was this moment. This near-electric current of passion was flooding back and forth between them and Rafe knew he couldn't wait one more second to claim her.

For more than a week, he'd watched her, laughed with her. He'd spent more time with Katie Charles in the last week than he had with his ex-wife in the last year of their marriage. And he'd enjoyed it more, as well. She was smart and funny and talented and so damn sexy; one look from her green eyes was almost enough to floor him.

She parted her thighs wider in acceptance and sighed as he touched her. Rafe felt the slam of that soft sound ricochet inside him and ignored it. He didn't want his heart to be involved in this, so it wouldn't be. He wouldn't allow any more connection than the physical between them. And that would be enough, he assured himself.

He just had to have her, and then everything would go back to normal.

Lifting her hips to give himself better access, he slowly pushed himself into her heat. Into the very heart of her. And as her body wrapped itself around his, he hissed in a breath and fought for control.

Instinctively, she moved with him, lifting her legs high enough to wrap them around his waist and pull him in deeper, tighter, harder. He looked down at her and she opened her arms to him. Leaning over, he kissed her as he rocked his body against hers. Retreating and then advancing, he felt the magical slide of her warmth and knew it had never been better for him.

For the first time in his adult life, he wished to hell he wasn't wearing a damn condom. He wanted to feel *all* of her, without that layer separating them. But that would have been nuts, so he pushed that thought aside and moved on her again.

She lifted up from the bed and kissed him, framing his face in her hands, running her tongue along his bottom lip until she pushed him so near the edge there was no restraining himself any longer. He'd wanted to draw this out. Wanted to make it last, because he'd been dreaming of this moment for days now. But there was no more waiting. No slow and seductive.

There was only need and the desperate ache for completion.

Pushing her back onto the bed, he levered himself over her and took her hard and fast.

"Yes," she whispered, moving with him, matching his rhythm eagerly. His body pistoned into hers. Her hunger fueled his and together they reached for what they both needed.

He felt her climax hit her and as she rode out the convulsing waves of pleasure, he erupted, called her name and joined her in time to slide into oblivion, locked together.

"My hero," Katie said when she was sure her voice would work.

"Happy to oblige," he murmured, his face tucked into the curve of her neck.

She smiled to herself and stared up at the pale blue ceiling overhead. The soft sigh of his breath against her skin, the heavy weight of his body pressing onto hers and the throbbing center of her where they were still joined all came together to create perfection.

Running her hands up and down his back, she listened to the sound of his ragged breathing and felt the pounding beat of his heart. It had been so long since she'd been with someone, that maybe she was making too much of this.

But there was a tiny voice inside her, whispering to Katie that this had been *special*. That she had just shared something with Rafe that went far beyond sex.

Her heartbeat jittered unsteadily as that thought settled into her mind. Hadn't she thought what she had with Cordell was special, too? But this was different, her thoughts argued. This was so much more than she had ever felt for Cordell. Rafe touched more than her heart. He'd somehow wormed his way into her soul.

But she was rushing things and she knew it. She wasn't going to be foolishly romantic about a purely physical pleasure. Not again. She wasn't in love, for heaven's sake. Katie was a rational, logical woman and she knew that falling in love just didn't happen in a week's time.

But she could at least admit that Rafe Cole was in her heart. She cared for him or she never would have slept with him. And watching him tonight with Nicole and Connor had only heightened her feelings for him. How could she *not* be touched by a man who was so gentle with a two-year-old? So nice to a single mom who had needed help?

Rafe was the kind of man she used to dream of finding. He was hardworking and honest and kind and so very, very sexy.

"You're thinking," he murmured.

"Yep," she said.

He lifted his head and quirked a smile at her. "Why is it that good sex energizes a woman and makes a man unconscious?"

"I'd tell you," she said solemnly, "but then I'd have to kill you."

He laughed and she felt the jolt of that movement ripple throughout her body. They were still locked together. Every move Rafe made awakened already sensitized flesh and set it sizzling.

"Hmm," he whispered, as if knowing exactly what she was thinking, feeling. He moved in her again, slowly at first, eliciting another sigh from Katie. "Seems we're not finished yet."

"Not nearly," she agreed, moving with him, sliding into the pace he set as if they had been together hundreds of times and knew each other's moves instinctively. It was, Katie thought, as if they had been meant to be together. As if their bodies had been forged specifically to link into place, two halves, one whole. She couldn't help feeling that this was all as it was supposed to be. That this night had been fated in some way. That she'd been given this chance with Rafe in order to make up for the wounded heart she'd lived through months before. And it was working.

In seconds, the fire between them was burning again. Flames licked at her center and spread throughout her body. He touched her and there was magic. He became a part of her body and a corner of her heart never wanted it to end.

She looked up into those deep blue eyes of his and thought how glad she was that she'd taken this chance with him. That she had opened herself up to possibilities. To the magic that could happen between the right people.

And then her thoughts splintered as he pushed her beyond desire into passion that demanded her focus. She felt the quickening within, the first tingle of anticipation that something amazing was about to happen. Katie reached for it eagerly, hungrily, wanting to feel it all again.

He kissed her and she opened her mouth to him, welcoming his invasion. The taste of him filled her and she felt his breath on her face. His body rocked into hers over and over again and she lifted her legs higher around his waist, holding him to her, offering herself up to his pleasure.

To *their* pleasure.

And when the first, shattering jolts hit her system, she

tore her mouth free of his, whispered his name and clung to him desperately. Moments later, while she shivered and trembled in his arms, he allowed himself to follow her and she held him tightly as his body exploded into hers.

Six

"That's it," he whispered. "Unconscious for real now."

"I feel great," she admitted with a happy sigh.

He looked down into her eyes and shook his head. "You're amazing."

"Why am I amazing?" she asked, reaching up to smooth his thick black hair off his forehead.

Studying her for a moment or two, he finally said, "Most women right now would be either regretting what just happened—"

"Not me," she said.

"—or they'd be silently planning how to make this a little more permanent."

Katie frowned and shook her head. "Also not me."

"I'm getting that," he said and rolled to one side of her, pulling her with him though, so that she rested her head on his shoulder.

Snuggling close, Katie listened to the steady beat of

his heart and the quiet, every-night noises of her old house. Wind rattled her windows and the familiar creaks and groans of the house settling sounded like whispers from friends.

She felt wonderful. Better than she had in too long to remember. But, she had heard what Rafe had to say and she knew he was probably right. A lot of women right now would be plotting how to keep him in their beds. In their lives. And, she had to admit, at least silently, that it would have been easy for her to fall into that category.

But she wasn't going to fool herself or tell herself comforting lies. She knew this one night wasn't the beginning of a "relationship." If not for remodeling her kitchen, she never would have met Rafe Cole. This wasn't your ordinary dating situation, she thought firmly. He hadn't made her any promises and she hadn't asked for any.

She rose up and braced her folded arms on his chest. Her hair was in her eyes, so she shook it back and looked at him squarely. Might as well have this conversation now, she told herself and gave him a sad smile.

"Uh-oh," he murmured. "That's not a this-was-great-let's-do-it-again smile, is it?"

"No," she told him and moved one hand to smooth his hair back from his forehead. If her fingers lingered a little longer than necessary, who was to know? "This was lovely, Rafe. Really. But—"

He frowned at her, did a quick roll and had her under him in the blink of an eye. Now he was looming over her and his blue gaze was fixed and sharp. "But *what?*"

She sighed. "I just don't think we should do this again, that's all."

"You're *dumping* me?"

"Well, we're not really a couple, so it's not really dumping you, but, yes. I guess so."

"I don't believe this." He sounded astonished and Katie admitted silently that he probably wasn't used to women turning him away. Any man who looked like he did had to have women clinging to him like cat hair. She chuckled a little at her pitiful analogy and his frown deepened.

"This is funny, too?"

"No, sorry." She stroked her hand up and down his arm, tracing the line of his well-defined muscles and barely restraining another sigh of appreciation. "No, this isn't funny. I just had a weird thought and—"

He snorted. "Perfect. So not only are you dumping me, but you can't even focus on the task?"

"Why are you getting angry?"

"Why the hell wouldn't I be?"

Katie felt a small spurt of irritation shoot through her. "Just a second ago, you were proud of me for not making more of this than there was."

"Yeah, but—"

"And now you're mad for the same reason?"

He blew out a breath and stared at her for a long second. "This isn't the usual response I get from women, so pardon the hell out of me if I'm a little surprised."

"Surprised, sure. But mad? Why?" Her minor irritation faded and she gave him a patient smile. "You feel the same way, you know you do. I just said it first. I would think you'd be glad for my reaction."

"Yeah, well, I'm not," he muttered, pulling away. He leaned back against the headboard and threw one arm behind his head. Giving her a look that probably should have worried her, he said, "So exactly what was tonight about, Katie?"

"Us," she said and scooted to sit beside him. Absently, she tugged the sheet up to cover her breasts. "We both wanted this, Rafe. And I thought, why shouldn't we have it?"

"And that's it?"

"Yes." Well, not completely of course, she thought. She did care for him and if she spent too much more time with him, she could come to care a lot more. Which would be a huge mistake. Yes, Rafe was a great guy, but she didn't trust herself anymore to know the good guys from the creeps.

Cordell King had seemed like a sweetie at first, too. Then he'd had a diamond bracelet overnighted to her along with a note saying they "were just too different to make a longer relationship work." Translation, she'd always known was really, *I'm rich, you're poor, goodbye.*

So, she'd been wrong about Cordell. And confidence in her character-reading skills was low. Nope. Better she bury herself in work for a year or two and then she'd get back out there. Oh, she was glad she'd had this night with Rafe. But she wasn't going to build a future out of it. Still, she knew now that she could get back into the world and one day she'd look for a man like Rafe, she told herself. Someone strong and kind and honest.

"I don't believe you," he said grimly. "Something else is going on here and I want to know what it is."

"Excuse me?"

"You heard me, Katie. You *like* me. I know you do. So why're you cutting me loose before the sheets are even cold?"

"That doesn't matter."

He grabbed her, pulled her across his lap and held her tightly to him. "Yeah. It does. To me."

Being this close to him really wasn't a good idea when she was trying to be logical and rational, Katie thought. She fought down the impulse to slide her palms across his broad, muscular chest and said, "You're taking this all wrong, Rafe."

"What did you expect? That I'd just get dressed, say thanks for the roll in the hay and then leave?"

"Well...*yes.*" Of course that's what she had expected. What man wouldn't enjoy free, no-strings-attached sex?

"Sorry to disappoint," he muttered, then tipped her chin up so that their gazes locked. "I want to know the real reason behind this."

"Rafe..."

"It's him, isn't it? The mysterious member of the King family."

Katie scowled at him, pulled free and scooted off his lap all at once. "If it is, that's my business."

"You just made it my business too, Katie. I'm getting the heave-ho because of this guy. The least you can do is tell me why."

"Because I trusted him, okay?" She blurted it out before she could stop herself and once the words started coming, there was no stopping them. "I thought I was in love with him. I thought he loved *me*. He was sweet and thoughtful and funny."

"And rich," Rafe muttered darkly. "Don't forget rich."

"Okay, yes, he was," she said. "But that's not why I fell in love with him. In fact, it's why it didn't work out in the end."

"What?"

Shaking her head, she pushed out of bed, walked to the connected bathroom and stepped inside. There she grabbed her bathrobe and pulled it on. When it was tied securely around her waist, she felt a little less vulnerable. Though the look in his eyes told her he wouldn't be leaving until he knew all of it. So she would be vulnerable anyway, she told herself. At least emotionally.

"Fine," she said at last. "You want the sad truth? He dropped me because we were too 'different.' Because I wasn't good enough. According to him our worlds were too far apart. Bottom line? Rich guy didn't want poor girl. Big surprise. There, happy now? Feel better getting *all* of my little humiliations up front?"

He simply stared at her. "Not good enough? Who the hell is he to say that about anybody?"

Unexpectedly, Katie smiled, despite the rawness of her feelings at the moment. His outrage on her behalf took a little of the sting out of her memories.

"He's a King," she said with a shrug she didn't quite feel. "Masters of the known universe. Just ask anyone. Heck, ask the guys you work with. They've probably got stories and complaints about the great King family."

He scowled at her. "Actually, the guys *like* working for King Construction. Haven't heard a word against them."

"Probably out of fear of losing their jobs," she muttered. On the other hand, maybe working for the King family was entirely different from trying to date one of them.

Frowning, he asked, "Who is he? Which King, I mean? Tell me who he is and I'll go punch him in the nose for you."

A surprised laugh shot from her throat and Katie was grateful for it. "Still my hero?"

"If you need one."

Tempting, she thought. He wasn't running for the hills. Maybe he was actually interested in her for more than a fleeting encounter. All she really had to do to find out was trust herself. Trust Rafe. She'd like to, Katie realized. But apparently she just wasn't ready.

Shaking her head, she said, "No, but thanks. I think I have to be my own hero first."

"So *you* want to punch him in the nose?"

She laughed louder. "Oh, I did, about six months ago. But I'm over it. I'm over *him*."

"No," he said, "you're not."

"Excuse me?"

He got out of bed and pulled on his jeans. "If you were over him, we wouldn't be having this conversation. We'd still be in bed, doing what we're obviously so good at."

Her amusement died in a flash. "This isn't about him. This is about me. It's about us."

He snorted and tugged on his boots. Then he grabbed his shirt off the floor, shrugged into it and stalked across the floor toward her. He stopped dead within arm's reach and then grabbed her, tugging her tightly to him. "You just told me there is no *us,* Katie, so get your stories straight."

"Let me go."

He did, but frustration simmered in the air around him. Shoving one hand through his hair, he grumbled, "What do you care what a King had to say anyway? Didn't that prove to you the man was an ass?"

"Don't you get it? I thought he was Prince Charming. Turned out he was a frog. But I never saw it." She threw both hands high and let them fall to her sides again. "How can I even trust my own judgment if I was that far off to begin with?"

"You're letting him win, Katie," he told her, bending over her, until their noses were practically brushing against each other. "By doubting yourself, you're giving that guy power he doesn't deserve."

"Maybe," she admitted. "But I'm not ready to make another mistake yet."

"What makes you so sure I'm a mistake?"

"I'm not sure," she told him quietly. "That's the problem."

He eased back a little, laid his hands on her shoulders and slowly drew them up until he held her face between his palms. His gaze was locked on her and Katie could have sworn his eyes were blue enough to drown in.

"You'll miss me."

"I know."

"I'm not going away," he said. "You'll see me every day."

"I know that, too."

Bending down, he kissed her, gently at first and then as the moments ticked past, the kiss deepened until Katie felt as though the ends of her hair were on fire. Finally though, Rafe pulled back to look at her again.

"Tonight isn't the end, Katie. It's just the beginning."

Before she could argue with him, he turned and walked out of the room.

When he got home, he placed a call.

"Sean?" he said when his brother answered. "Did you get hold of Garrett?"

"No can do," Sean said. "He's in Ireland and he's not answering his phone."

"Ireland?" Rafe repeated. "What's he doing over there?"

"Exactly the question I asked his twin. Griffin says Jefferson had some problems with a thief in his European company and Garrett went to investigate it."

Great timing, Rafe thought in disgust. Jefferson King, one of their many cousins, lived with his Irish wife on a sheep farm in County Mayo. Hard to believe that Jefferson, Mr. Hollywood Mogul, was happy out in the boonies, but he was. And if Jeff had a problem, then there was no telling when Garrett might come back home. To the Kings, *Family comes first* was the unofficial motto. So Garrett wouldn't leave Ireland until he'd turned the country upside down to find the answers Jeff wanted.

"Well, that's great," Rafe grumbled, stalking through the sleek, modern hotel suite he called home. The place was empty, of course, but tonight, it felt…desolate. Rafe had always preferred life in a hotel. It was easy. Uncomplicated. But tonight, it also felt…sterile.

His mind kept returning to Katie's older house with its overstuffed furniture and creaky floors. There was a sense of continuity in that bungalow, as if the walls and floors themselves held the echoes of generations of laughter and tears.

His gaze swept the interior of his own home and for the first time in years, he found it lacking. Irritated with himself, he opened the sliding glass door to his terrace and stepped outside. The cold wind slapped at him and the roar of the ocean growled unceasingly. Streetlamps below threw yellowed circles of light onto the sidewalks and out on the beach. He spotted the dancing flames of campfires blazing in the fire rings.

"So," he asked, "we still don't have any idea which one of the family is the one who messed with Katie."

"Nope," Sean said. "Not a clue. And except for the married ones, it could be anyone."

"This I know already." Rafe shoved one hand through his hair and squinted into the cold sea breeze. His body was still humming from his time with Katie, and his mind was racing, trying to figure out how it had all gone to hell so damn fast.

He didn't have an answer.

"I can ask around," Sean offered.

"Never mind," Rafe told him. "I'll do the asking myself."

"Fine," Sean said, then asked, "Hey, did you get me some cookies?"

Rafe hung up, stuffed his phone into his pocket, then leaned both hands on the wrought-iron railing in front of him. He leaned into the wind, watched the black waves moving and shifting in the moonlight and promised himself that he would find out who had hurt Katie.

A few days later, Rafe was still simmering. He was getting nowhere fast with talking to his cousins. Amazing how many Kings took off during the summer. What the hell had happened to the family's work ethic? But it wasn't just the frustration of trying to find out which of his cousins he should pummel that was making him insane.

It was Katie herself. Until her, the only woman who'd ever turned her back on him was Leslie. And at least she had *married* him first.

"Everything okay here?"

Rafe buried his irritation, turned the electric sander off and faced Joe, the man pretending to be his boss. "Fine," Rafe said shortly and moved the finished cabinet door to one side before grabbing up the next one in line.

Sanding was hot, tedious work, so his mind had plenty of room to wander. Unfortunately, it continued to wander toward Katie.

The woman was making him insane and that had never happened before. Always in his life, Rafe was in charge. He did what he wanted when he wanted and didn't much care about looking out for whoever might be in his way. Since Leslie, women were expendable in his world. Temporary. They came in, spent a few good hours with him; then they were gone, not even leaving behind a residual echo of their presence.

"Until now," he muttered, removing the safety goggles and paper mask he wore to avoid inhaling all the sawdust flying around so thickly in the air.

Joe glanced over his shoulder to make sure no one was close enough to overhear them. "Look, I don't know what's going on, but I just came from talking to Katie and she's wound so tight she's giving off sparks."

"Really?" Rafe hid a smile. Good to know he wasn't the only one. She had managed to avoid talking to him the last few days, so he hadn't known exactly how she was feeling until just this moment. It had about killed him to be here, so near to her every damn day, and not speak to her. Touch her. But he'd kept his distance because damned if he'd be the one to bend. He wanted her. She knew it. Let her come to him. She was, after all, the one who pushed him away to begin with. "She say anything?"

"She didn't have to," Joe told him. "The whole time I was talking to her about her new floor tiles, she kept looking out here at *you*."

Also good to know, Rafe thought and hid a satisfied smile.

"What's going on?"

Rafe slanted a hard look at Joe. He'd known the man for years. Trusted him. Considered him a friend, even. But that didn't mean that he was interested in Joe's opinion on this particular subject. "That's none of your business, is it?"

The older man scrubbed one hand across the top of his balding head. "No, I guess it's not. But I work for King Construction. I've got a good reputation with the company and with our clients."

"You do," Rafe said, keeping his voice down. "What's your point?"

"I've known you a long time, Rafe, and I'm going to say that my business or not, I think you need to tell that girl who you really are."

He snorted. "Not likely."

Hell, she'd kicked him loose thinking he was Rafe *Cole*. If she knew he was actually a King, who knew what she'd do?

Joe huffed out an impatient breath. "She's a nice woman and I don't like the idea of lying to her. I'm sorry I suggested this bet in the first place."

Rafe saw how uncomfortable Joe was and he was sorry for that. But he wasn't telling Katie the truth. Not yet. Not until he'd made her see how much she wanted him. How much she liked him. Then he'd tell her that she was wrong about the King family and him specifically. And she'd have to admit that she had made a mistake.

"Look, Joe," he said, "I'm sorry you're in the middle of this, but we're already too deep in the game to stop. There's no changing the rules at this late date."

"A game? Is that what this is?" Joe's eyes narrowed and Rafe had the distinct impression that his contractor was about to defend Katie's honor.

Well, there was no need.

"I don't mean Katie is a game to me, so relax."

The man's pitbull expression eased a bit and Rafe kept talking.

"Don't get all twisted up over this, Joe." Rafe slapped one hand on the man's shoulder. "We made the bet and I'm honoring it. As for telling Katie the truth, I'll do that when the time's right."

"And when's that?"

"Not now, for damn sure." Rafe narrowed his own eyes in warning. "And don't you tell her, either."

Grumbling under his breath, Joe worked his jaw furiously as if there were a hundred hot words in his mouth that he was fighting to keep inside. Finally though, he grudgingly agreed. "Fine. I won't say anything. But I think you're making a mistake here, Rafe. One that you're gonna regret real soon."

"Maybe," he said and shifted his gaze back to the enclosed patio where Katie was working in her temporary kitchen. Even from a distance, she was beautiful, he thought. But it wasn't just her beauty calling to him. It was the shine of something tender in her eyes. The knowledge that she had wanted him, desired him, without knowing who he was. She didn't want anything from him and that was so rare in Rafe's world that he couldn't let her go.

But his heart wasn't involved here and it wouldn't be, either. He had tried love. Tried marriage and failed miserably at both. Kings didn't fail. It was the one rule his father had drummed into all of them from the time they were kids.

Well, his divorce from Leslie was going to be the *only* time Rafe King failed at anything. He wouldn't risk another mistake. Wouldn't give Fate another shot at kicking his ass.

"Whether or not I regret anything," Rafe told Joe quietly, "is not your business. You just do your job and leave Katie Charles to me."

"Fine. You're the boss," Joe said after a long minute of silence. "But King or not, you're making a mistake."

Joe walked off to the kitchen where Steve and Arturo were jokingly arguing about the plastering job. Inside her temporary kitchen, Katie was busy working on another batch of her cookies and the delicious aromas wafting from the oven wrapped themselves around him. Rafe stood alone in the sunlight while his mind raced with possibilities.

Maybe Joe had a point. But being with Katie, keeping his identity a secret, didn't feel like a mistake to Rafe. So he was going to stick with his original plan. Once a decision had been made, Rafe never liked to deviate. That was second-guessing himself and if he started doing that, where would it end? No.

Better he take the fall for his own decisions than have to pay for unsolicited advice gone wrong.

Seven

Emily O'Hara was waiting for Rafe outside Katie's house late that afternoon. Again, he was the last man to leave and he had lingered even later than usual, half hoping Katie would get back from the store before he left. He wanted to talk to her. Hell, he admitted silently, that wasn't all he wanted.

Since Katie wasn't home, he was surprised to find her grandmother leaning against his truck when he walked out front to leave. She wore a hot-pink oversize shirt over a white tank top and white pants. Huge red-framed sunglasses shielded her eyes, but when she heard him approach, she pushed them up to the top of her head.

Idly filing her nails, she looked up at him as he got closer and gave him a tight smile that should have warned him something was up. But, he reminded himself, if there was one thing Rafe knew, it was women. Granted, he didn't have much experience with older females, but how hard could it be to pour on some charm and win her over?

Besides, Katie's grandmother had seemed nice enough when he first met her. What could possibly go wrong?

"Mrs. O'Hara," he said, giving her a guileless smile designed to put her at her ease, "Katie's not home."

"Oh, I know that Rafe. It's Tuesday. My girl always goes grocery shopping on Tuesdays. I've tried to shake up her world a little, but she does love a schedule." She straightened up, tucked her emery board into the oversize purse hanging from her shoulder and cocked her head to look at him. "Wait, maybe I shouldn't call you Rafe at all. Maybe you'd prefer it if I call you Mr. King?"

Rafe flinched and a sinking sensation opened up in the pit of his stomach. This he hadn't expected at all. She knew who he was. Had she told Katie? No, he thought. If she had, he'd have heard about it by now. Hell, Katie would have come at him with both barrels blazing. So the question was, why hadn't her grandmother given him up?

"Rafe'll do," he told her and stuffed his hands into his pockets. "How long have you known who I am?"

She chuckled. "Since the moment my Katie introduced you as Rafe Cole." Shaking her head, she ran one finger along the hood of the truck, looked at the dirt she'd picked up, then clucked her tongue and rubbed her fingers together to get rid of it.

"See, Katie's a good girl, but she's single-minded. At the moment, she's so focused on her business that she doesn't see anything else. Sadly, her pop culture knowledge is lacking, too. If she'd read the celebrity magazines more often, as I do..." She paused to give him another one of those cool, measuring stares. "Then she would have recognized you, too. Though I will say, you look different in jeans than you do in a tux at some fancy party."

Inwardly, he groaned. Stupid. He hadn't even thought of that. He'd been in one of those weekly tabloidesque magazines only last month. Photographers at the Save the Shore benefit had gotten shots of him squiring an actress to the affair. Not that he and Selena were a couple or anything. After one date, he'd known that a man could only talk hairdos and tanning tips for so long.

Sliding his hands from his pockets, he folded his arms over his chest in a classic defense posture. Emily might appear to be a sweet older lady, but the glint in her eye told him that he'd better walk soft and careful. But Rafe was used to sometimes-hostile negotiations with suppliers, so he was as prepared for this confrontation as he could be. Bracing his feet wide apart, he waited for whatever was coming next.

"So, not going to deny it at least," she said.

"What would be the point?"

"There is that."

Curious now, Rafe asked, "Why haven't you told Katie?"

"Interesting question," Emily acknowledged with a small smile. "I've asked that of myself a time or two in the last couple of weeks. But the truth is, I wanted to wait and see what you were up to first."

"And?"

"Still waiting." She wagged her finger at him as if he were a ten-year-old boy. She took a step or two away from the truck, walking from sunlight into shade. Her sandals clicked on the concrete driveway. When she turned to look at him again she asked, "So instead of keeping me in suspense, why don't you do us both a favor and tell me what's going on? Why are you pretending to be someone you're not?"

For one moment, Rafe caught himself wondering what it might have been like to have a woman like this one in his life. He had the distinct impression she would be a lioness when protecting Katie. He couldn't blame her for that, Rafe thought, even as he shrugged. He didn't want to be disrespectful, but damned if he'd explain himself to Katie's grandmother, either.

"Long story short," he offered, "I lost a bet so I'm working this job. Easier to work it as a nobody than one of the bosses."

"That explains why you haven't told your crew," she said thoughtfully. "It doesn't explain lying to Katie."

"No, it doesn't."

She blew out an impatient breath and prompted, "And? So?"

One look in the woman's eyes, so much like her granddaughter's, told Rafe that she wasn't going to give up until she had what she'd come here for. He didn't like being put on the spot. Didn't appreciate having to justify his actions. But, if there was one thing Rafe respected, it was loyalty and he could see that feeling ran deep in this woman.

So, though he wouldn't explain himself thoroughly, he was willing to give her the bare bones. "I like her. She hates the Kings. So I'm not about to tell her I'm one of them."

"Ever?" Emily asked, clearly dumbfounded.

"I'll have to tell her eventually," he acknowledged, "but in my own time and my own way."

"And when is that, exactly?"

Looking into her eyes, Rafe wondered why he had considered this woman to be just a nice older lady. Katie's nana had steel in her spine. He wasn't used to this. Rafe couldn't even remember the last time anyone had questioned him about anything. He was a King. He didn't do explanations or apologies. And he didn't, for damn sure, wither under a disapproving stare from a suburban grandmother.

Yet, that was just what he was doing.

"When I've convinced her that not *all* Kings are bastards," he admitted. "When she likes me enough, I'll tell her everything, prove to her she was wrong about us and then I'll get out of her life."

Emily blinked at him, then shook her head as if she hadn't heard him right. "That's your plan?"

"Something wrong with it?"

"Let me count the ways," she muttered, with yet another shake of her head.

He didn't care what she thought of his plan, he was sticking with it. But as he stood there, another idea occurred to him and he wondered why he hadn't thought of it before. Could have saved himself, and his brother Sean, a lot of trouble. Taking a step or two closer to Emily, he said, "You know which of the Kings treated her badly, right?"

She frowned so harshly, Rafe was instantly glad it wasn't *him* this formidable woman was mad at. "I do."

"Tell me," he said shortly. "Tell me who he is. I'm trying to find out, but it's taking me too long."

"Why do you care?"

"Because—" Rafe's mouth snapped shut. He took a breath and said, "I want to know who hurt her so I can hurt him back."

"One of your own family?"

He heard the surprise in her voice and a part of him shared it. The Kings always stuck together. It was practically a vow they all took at birth. It was the King cousins against the world and God help anyone who tried to undermine them. The occasional brawls and fistfights notwithstanding, none of the Kings had ever turned on another.

"Yeah," he said, realizing that cousin or not, Rafe really wanted to hit the guy responsible for Katie's defensiveness. No matter who the King cousin—or brother—was, Rafe was going to make him sorry for hurting Katie.

"Again," Emily said quietly, "I have to ask, why do you care?"

He scrubbed one hand across the back of his neck and gritted his teeth in frustration. Rafe wasn't sure himself why he cared so damn much, he only knew he did. The only possible explanation was that he didn't like the idea of a woman like Katie hating the Kings. She was…nice. Frowning at that moronic thought, he grumbled aloud, "You ask a hell of a lot of questions."

"I do indeed. So how about an answer?" she countered. "An honest one."

Rafe met her gaze and wondered if Katie would be as amazing a woman as her grandmother when she was Emily's age. He had to figure that she would. As the Kings were always saying, *it's in the blood*. And a part of him wanted to be around to see Katie as a scary-smart old woman. He dismissed that thought quickly enough though, as he knew all too well that commitment and permanence weren't in him.

Choosing his words carefully, Rafe said, "Honestly, I don't know why I care so much. I only know I do. I don't like knowing it was one of my family who caused her pain. And I don't like knowing she hates the Kings because of that one jerk—whoever he is. So give me a name and I'll take care of it and get out of Katie's life all that much sooner."

She gave him a slow, wide smile and shook her head firmly enough to have her short, silver hair lifting in the breeze. "You know what? I don't think I will."

"Why not?"

"Because, I'd rather watch you play out your plan," she admitted. "My Katie can take care of herself, you know. That guy hurt her, but he didn't break her. You know why? Because she only *thought* she was in love. You might want to remember that, Rafe."

Confusion rose up inside him, but he swallowed it back. "Fine, I'll remember."

"Good. Now, I've got a hot date, so I've got to get a move on," she announced and turned around to leave, only to whirl back to face him again. Pointing at him, she said, "Just one more thing."

"What's that?"

Her eyes narrowed and her voice dropped a couple of notches. There wasn't even the glimmer of a smile on her face. "If you break her heart, I'll hunt you down like a sick dog and make you sorry you ever set foot in Katie's house. Sound fair?"

Rafe nodded, admiration for the older woman filling him again. Family loyalty he understood completely. And he found himself again envying Katie for having someone in her life who loved her so much.

He'd never known that himself. Oh, he had his brothers and cousins, sure. His mother, though, hadn't loved him; she'd only used him as a bargaining chip, to squeeze Ben King for money. The elderly aunt who'd raised him hadn't—she'd only done her duty, as she often told him. Rafe was pretty sure his father had loved him, as much as Ben King was able. Rafe wasn't feeling sorry for himself. Things were as they were. And he'd done fine on his own.

But he had to wonder how it might have been to be raised with the kind of love he saw now, glittering in Emily O'Hara's eyes.

"I hear you."

"Good." She set her sunglasses in place, flashed him a quick smile and said, "As long as we understand each other, we'll be fine."

Then she waved one hand and hurried to a bright yellow VW bug parked at curbside. She hopped in, fired it up and was gone an instant later.

Scowling to himself, Rafe looked back at Katie's house, quiet in the afternoon light. The crew was gone, *she* was gone and the old bungalow looked as empty as he felt.

Talking to Emily had shaken him. Hearing his own plan put into words had made him realize that maybe it was as dumb as Katie's grandmother clearly thought it was. The lie he'd spun and invested so much in suddenly felt like a weight around his neck. He had to wonder if he wasn't doing the wrong thing in keeping it going.

He'd started this as a way to win her affection and respect without her knowing who he really was. But if he pulled it off, what did he really gain? She wasn't caring for the real him if she didn't *know* the real man. The sad truth was, Katie now cared about a lie. A fabrication. He'd done this to himself and couldn't see a way out without risking everything he didn't want to lose.

Rafe didn't like admitting it even to himself, but he suddenly felt more alone than he ever had in his life. And he wasn't sure what the hell to do about it.

* * *

Katie had deliveries to make bright and early the next morning. Any other day, she would have enjoyed being the one to drop off a surprise gift of cookies. She always got a charge out of seeing people's reactions to the elegantly frosted and wrapped creations. Since she'd become busier, she didn't normally have time to make deliveries herself anymore.

Usually, she had a teenager from down the street deliver her cookie orders. It helped her out and Donna made more money than she would babysitting. A win-win situation all the way around.

But Donna was on vacation with her family, so despite being so tired she could barely stand up, Katie had no choice but to load up her car with the week's orders. Specially made boxes lined her trunk and she carefully stored away the cookie bouquets and cookie towers and cookie cakes that she'd spent the last two days making. Each of them were frosted, some personalized and a swell of pride filled her as she looked at them.

She'd built this business out of nothing and she had big plans for it, too.

"And that," she told herself firmly, "is just one more reason to stay away from Rafe."

He was too male. Too overwhelming to every sense she possessed. She couldn't afford to be distracted from her goals, not even by a man who had the ability to sweep her off her feet with a single glance. And, if she hadn't already surrendered to her own hormones, he wouldn't be taking up so much of her thoughts. So she deliberately stopped thinking about Rafe—though it wasn't easy.

For now, she would devote herself to her burgeoning business. She wanted to make an even bigger name for herself. Move Katie's Kookies into a shop down on Pacific Coast Highway. Have several ovens, hire more help, expand her client list and maybe even go into online orders. She had big plans. And nothing was going to stop her from making them come true.

The scents of vanilla, cinnamon and chocolate filled her car and made Katie smile in spite of the fact that she was running on about three hours sleep. But she couldn't blame her sleeplessness entirely on the fact that she'd been baking half the night. Because when she finally did get to bed, she'd slept fitfully, tortured by dreams of Rafe. Of the night they'd had together.

And there he was again, front and center in her brain. Seeing him every day wasn't helping her avoid thoughts of him. Especially since her own body seemed determined to remind her, every chance it got, of just what she'd experienced in his arms.

"Need some help?"

Katie jolted and slapped one hand to her chest as she turned around to look at the very man she had just been thinking about. "You scared me."

"Sorry." He grinned. "I called out to you, but you didn't hear me, I guess."

No, she hadn't. She'd been too busy remembering his hands on her skin. The taste of his mouth. The slow slide of his body invading hers. Oh, boy. She blew out a breath, forced a smile and said, "I'm just preoccupied."

"I can see that," he said, glancing into the back of the SUV. "You've been busy."

"I really have," she admitted, and turned to pick up the last box, holding a dozen pink frosted cookies shaped like baby rattles.

"Let me get that," he said and reached for it before she could stop him.

Truthfully, even though it was a little uncomfortable being around him at the moment, Katie was glad he was there. She'd spent the last few days avoiding being alone with him, allowing herself only a glimpse of him now and then. Having him close enough now that she could feel his body heat was a sort of tempting torture. He looked great in his worn blue jeans and blue T-shirt with King Construction stenciled across the back. And he smelled even better, with the scent of soap from his morning shower still clinging to his skin. She wanted to go to him. To kiss him.

She caught that thought and strangled it. She was so tired, she was nearly staggering. Way too tired to trust her instincts around a man she already knew she wanted. Katie gave herself a quick, silent talking-to. Besides, she still had a full morning of deliveries.

"Thanks."

He set the box in the trunk, then shot her a look. "Are you okay?"

"Yes. Just tired."

He frowned and shifted his gaze to the mass of cookies. "You're delivering all of these yourself?"

She yawned and nodded. "Sorry. Yes. My usual delivery girl is camping in Yosemite with her family so…"

"You can hardly keep your eyes open," he accused.

As if to prove him wrong, Katie opened her eyes as wide as possible and pretended not to notice that they felt like marbles rolling in sand. "I'm fine. Really. I'll have these done in an hour or two and then I'll come home and take a nap."

From inside the kitchen, a saw buzzed into life.

"Well, maybe I'll take a nap," she said with a wry smile.

He didn't return the smile. Instead, he glowered at her, crossed his arms over his chest and said flatly, "You're not driving anywhere."

She blinked at him. "Excuse me?"

Shaking his head, Rafe said, "Katie, you're practically asleep on your feet. You try to drive and you'll end up killing someone. Or yourself."

"You're overreacting," she said and closed the trunk lid. "I can take care of myself."

"Sure you can," he agreed amiably. "When you're awake."

"I'm not your responsibility, Rafe," she argued, fighting the urge to yawn again. See? Just another reason why they wouldn't have worked out as a couple. He was too bossy and she was too stubborn.

God, she was tired. Another yawn sneaked up on her before she could stifle it and she saw his eyes narrow dangerously. Perfect. She had just given him more ammunition for his argument. To head him off before he could say anything, she spoke up quickly. "Look, I appreciate the concern, really. But I'm fine and we both have work to do. Why don't we just get on with what we were doing and let this go?"

"I don't think so." Rafe grabbed the keys from the trunk lock and held them out of reach. "I'm not kidding about this. No way am I letting you drive."

"Letting me?" she repeated incredulously as she stared up into his implacable expression. "You don't have a vote in it, Rafe. This is my car. My business, and I say I'm fine to drive."

"You're wrong." He looked over his shoulder at the house. "Wait here."

He might as well have patted her on the head and ordered her to *stay.* As if she were a golden retriever or something. And of course she would wait there. What choice did she have? Katie wondered in irritation. He'd taken her keys.

Anger churned inside her and mixed with the fatigue clawing at her. Probably not a good combination. Okay. Fine. Yes, she really *was* exhausted. But she wasn't a danger to people on the road for heaven's sake. She wasn't a complete idiot. She wouldn't drive if she didn't think she could.

The longer he was gone, the more irritated she became. She paced—in the garage, muttering to herself, rubbing her gritty eyes. One night with the man and he became territorial. Probably a good idea she'd decided to keep her distance. Imagine what he'd be like if they were actually in a relationship.

Then that thought settled in. Instead of making her angrier, it gave Katie a soft, warm glow. Who was she kidding? She'd love for someone to be that worried about her. Oh, not that she was some mindless woman to take orders from anyone. But the idea that a man would care enough to worry about her safety sort of dulled the edges of her anger. Of course, she thought wryly, that could be the exhaustion talking.

So when he finally came back, her tone hadn't softened by much as she said, "Give me my keys."

"Not a chance." He took her arm in a firm, no-nonsense grip, steered her to the passenger side of her car, opened the door and said simply, "Get in."

Stubbornly, Katie pulled free of his hold and took a determined step back. Standing her ground, she lifted her chin in defiance and met him stare for stare. "This isn't funny, Rafe."

His blue eyes narrowed on her. "Damn right it isn't. You're too self-sufficient for your own good."

"What's that supposed to mean?"

"It means that you're so focused on doing everything on your own you don't know enough to ask for help when you need it." He scowled at her as if expecting her to quail before his impeccable logic.

She didn't.

"I don't need help, and if I did, I wouldn't come to you."

He took a quick, sharp breath. "Why the hell not?"

"Because, we're not together and you're supposed to be working on my kitchen."

"We could be together if you weren't so damn hard-headed," he pointed out. "And as for working on your kitchen, I can do that when we get back."

"*We* aren't going anywhere," she argued and felt another yawn sneaking up on her. She twisted her mouth together and clamped her lips shut rather than giving into it.

"Nice try, but I saw that yawn anyway," he pointed out.

"Doesn't mean a thing," she told him.

"Damn it, Katie," Rafe said, his voice quiet, his gaze locked on hers, "Even if you don't want *my* help, you could at least admit that you're too damn tired to think straight, let alone drive."

He was leaning on the open passenger door, just an arm's reach away from her. His blue eyes were locked on her and his dark blue, steely stare told Katie he wouldn't be giving up easily.

So she tried another tactic.

"Rafe," she assured him in a calm, rational tone that completely belied the irritation still spiking inside her, "I'm completely fine. Really."

Then she yawned again.

"Uh-huh," he said, "I'm convinced. Get in. I'm driving."

"You?" She looked from him to the kitchen, where the crew was busy doing heaven knew what to her house and asked, "You can't just walk away from your job."

"I told the guys to let Joe know I was helping you out and that I'd be back in a couple of hours."

"You can't do that." Wouldn't he be fired? She couldn't let him lose his job over this.

"Yeah," he said, "I can. Consider us a full-service construction company. Whatever the boss—that's *you*—needs, we provide."

Katie hadn't gone to him, he'd come to her. And there was the slightest chance that he was right and she was too tired to drive all over town. But at the same time, that didn't make it okay for him to ride in and take over.

She thought about it, her mind racing, arguing with itself. Yes, he was being a jerk, but he was also being nice, in a roundabout, tyrannical sort of way. He was glaring at her, but he was worried about her. He was supposed to be working on her kitchen, but instead he was willing to drive her around town making cookie deliveries.

And she would be alone with him in the car for an hour or more. That appealed to her on so many levels it was scary. But could she really be with him and *not* with him at the same time?

Oh, she was so tired, even *she* didn't understand her any more.

"I can practically hear you arguing with yourself," he said after a long moment.

"It's easier than arguing with you," she told him.

"True. And before we start in again, you should know that I don't quit. I don't give in. Never surrender."

She tipped her head to one side and looked up at him. "I don't quit, either."

He shrugged. "Hence the trouble between us."

"Hence?" she repeated, smiling in spite of the situation.

Rafe blew out a breath. "Are you getting in, or do I pick you up and *put* you in?" he asked.

Katie sent him a hard glare. "All right, fine," she confessed. "I *might* be a little too tired to drive."

He smiled and Katie's toes curled in her comfortable flats. Oh, boy. For all of her fine notions about keeping her distance, about not letting herself fall for a guy, she was certainly doing a lot of stumbling around him.

"Now that we're on the same page, so to speak," Rafe said, "will you please get in the car?"

Her mouth twitched into a smile at the way he'd changed his command to a request. She nodded, climbing up into the passenger seat. "Thank you."

"You're welcome." He closed her door, walked around to the driver's side and slid her key into the ignition. Then he looked at her and said, "So, how does it feel to be going on our second date?"

Her eyebrows winged up when she turned her gaze on him. "Delivering cookies is a date?"

"If we say it is, yeah." He fired up the engine and looked at her again. "So? Is it?"

Katie stared at him and remembered that night. Then she remembered the last few days, being so close to him and so far away all at the same time. She remembered every haunting dream she'd had and how she would wake up, aching for his touch.

Was she being an idiot by shutting out the first nice,

normal guy she'd met in way too long? Okay, yes, he was a little bossy, but she could handle that. Would it really be so bad to take a chance? To spend some time with Rafe? To see if what she already felt for him might grow? After all, she could concentrate on her business *and* have a life, couldn't she? Isn't that what Nana and Nicole both had been trying to tell her?

Memories of Cordell rose up in her mind, but Katie fought them down with determination.

Watching Rafe, she finally said, "It's not a date unless you spring for a cup of coffee at least."

He grinned at her, clearly victorious. "One latte, coming up."

Eight

An hour and a half later, Katie looked a little more alert and Rafe was enjoying himself immensely. "No wonder you like doing this," he said, sliding into the driver's seat after making the last of the deliveries. "People are excited to see you when you bring them cookies."

She grinned. "How did the pink baby-rattle cookies go over?"

He laughed and held up a five-dollar bill. "I got a tip!"

He looked so pleased with himself, Katie had to laugh, too. "Congratulations, you're a delivery person."

"She cried, too," he said, handing Katie the five. Shaking his head, he remembered the expression on the woman's face when she opened the door and saw him standing there, holding the basket of pink frosted cookies. "The woman? The new mom? She took one look at those cookies her friend ordered from you and burst into tears. She was laughing and crying and for a minute." Then he added, "it was terrifying."

Katie reached out and patted his arm. "Not what you're used to as a carpenter?"

"No," he said simply, looking into her green eyes. She was so pleased with him, having so much fun, he couldn't help but suddenly feel like a first-class rat for lying to her.

He thought back to his conversation with Katie's grandmother and realized that she had been right. Ever since talking to Emily, he'd been rethinking this whole keep-the-lie-going thing. His lies hadn't seemed like such a big deal when he had started out on this job. But now, every day with Katie made him feel that much more like a jerk. He should have told her the truth before now.

Sure, he'd told Emily that he was sticking to his plan, but she'd made him start to doubt the wisdom in that. But he couldn't think of a good way out of this mess. Because, he realized with startling clarity, the moment he told Katie about his lies, what his real name was, it would all be over between them.

Odd that he hadn't considered that possibility before. But then, he hadn't thought that he would *want* to keep seeing her once this job was finished. Now though, he knew he didn't want her disappearing from his life at the end of this job. He wanted to keep seeing her. And the chances of that happening looked slim.

He imagined blurting out the truth right there and then. Telling her that he wasn't the man she thought he was. And in his mind's eye, he saw her features tighten with betrayal, saw the shine in her green eyes dim and then flash with fury, and he told himself that it didn't matter if he was starting to get uncomfortable with his lies.

She wasn't ready to learn the truth.

He wanted her to care for him before he told her who he was. And then? a voice in his mind whispered. But he didn't have an answer to that yet. All Rafe knew was that he wanted to be with her *now*. And he didn't want the King name ruining that.

So he was stuck with his lies, his plan, whether he wanted to be or not.

"How are you feeling?" he asked, suddenly changing the subject.

"A little more awake, thanks. The latte helped."

"Not enough," he decided. Her green eyes were shadowed and her face was too pale to suit him. The fact that he was worried about her bothered him, but there didn't seem to be anything he could do about that. "You still look tired."

"Well, don't I feel pretty?" she asked wryly.

"You're beautiful." Two words, softly spoken, and they seemed to echo in the air around them. He hadn't meant to blurt that out. It had been a knee-jerk reaction.

"Rafe—"

"Don't," he said quietly, before she could start in on her speech about how nothing had changed and she still wasn't interested in being with him. He could *feel* her reaction to his closeness. Her skin was warm and though her eyes were tired, he still noticed the gleam of desire in their depths.

Leaning in closer to her, Rafe reached out, touched her cheek with his fingertips and tipped her face up for his kiss. "Just, let me…"

She sighed and moved into him, meeting him halfway, taking what he offered, and Rafe was relieved. He didn't know if he could have taken her turning from him or pulling away. He'd been thinking about doing just this for the last few days. Thinking about *her*. The first touch of her mouth to his eased everything inside him, yet rekindled a fire that had been nothing more than glowing embers since their one night together.

His body tightened, his heartbeat thundered in his chest and Rafe had to fight every instinct he possessed to keep from grabbing her and yanking her close to him. He wanted his hands on her again. Wanted her under him, over him. Wanted her body surrendering to his.

He groaned then, knowing he couldn't have everything he wanted right now. And the longer he kissed her, the less willing he would be to stop. So he pulled back while he still could and drew a long, shaky breath.

Resting his forehead against hers, he waited for control to slide back into his body, but it was a long time coming. Especially when he could feel her short, sharp breaths against his face. Well, he thought wryly, so much for her claims of not wanting to be with him again.

Several long moments passed before he gave her a smile, looked into her eyes and said, "There. Told you we weren't done with each other."

Katie shook her head, one corner of her mouth tipping into a reluctant half smile. "You really think now is the right time for I-told-you-sos?"

"What better time?"

"You're impossible."

"I like that." He skimmed his fingers through her hair until his hand was at the back of her neck, kneading her skin with a sure, gentle touch.

"You would," she told him, sighing at his touch.

"Are we going to argue again?" he asked. "Because I warn you, I'm getting to the point where I really enjoy our 'disagreements.'"

"Maybe later." She cupped his cheek in the palm of her hand.

"At least you admit there will be a 'later.'"

"Yes," she said with a slow nod, never tearing her gaze from his. "There will be."

"Tonight." Rafe caught her hand in his. "I want to see you tonight."

"Okay," she said. "Another barbecue?"

"Oh, I think this time we'll let someone else cook. I'll pick you up at seven," he said, easing back behind the wheel.

"To go where?"

"That's a surprise." He shot her a quick grin as a plan formed in his mind while he steered the car into traffic. "All you have to do is dress up. Oh, and take a nap. I want you wide awake tonight."

"That sounds intriguing."

"Count on it."

His mind was already racing with plans and he smiled to himself as it all began to come together.

That feeling lasted until he went home to change.

The minute he walked into his hotel suite, he knew someone was there. Didn't take a genius, after all. There was a designer purse on his couch and a pair of black heels under the glass-topped coffee table.

Rafe's brain raced frantically. Had he already set up a date for tonight? He didn't think so. Hell, he hadn't seen anyone since Selena the Self Involved Actress. So who...?

"Rafe? Is that you?"

The familiar, feminine voice sent a twist of old pain mixed with regret slashing through his middle, but he fought it down and managed to give his ex-wife a half smile when she came in off the balcony.

"Leslie. What are you doing here?"

The cool, elegant brunette flashed him a brief, wry smile. "Well, good to see you too, Rafe."

Irritated at being called to the carpet on his manners when she was the one who'd shown up unannounced and let herself into *his* home, Rafe just stared at her. Waiting.

It didn't take long. Leslie never had been the patient type. "I know I should have called before just showing up here."

"That would've been good," he said.

She stood with the balcony and the bank of windows at her back. Rafe was absolutely sure she knew that the sunlight streaming in through those windows was highlighting her to a beautiful advantage. Leslie always had known how to show herself off in the best way. She was lovely, self-assured and the only woman in the world who had ever told him that he wasn't good enough.

That memory colored his tone when he spoke. "How did you get in here?"

"Oh," she said, giving him a palms-up shrug, "Declan's still the concierge here. He let me up so I could wait for you in private."

Silently, Rafe told himself that he'd be having a little chat with Declan real soon. For the moment though… "I repeat. What are you doing here?"

Leslie frowned slightly, not enough to mar her brow or anything, but he got the message. She had never had any trouble letting Rafe know that he'd disappointed her in some way. Looking back now, he couldn't even remember *why* they had gotten married in the first place.

"You always were a straightforward man," she murmured.

"As I recall, that's one of the things you didn't care for."

Her mouth flattened into a straight line briefly; then, as if she'd willed it to happen, it curved again slightly. "Look at us. It's been years since we divorced and we're still treating each other like the enemy."

He shifted a little at that, since it was true and there really was no point in it. Leslie wasn't a part of his life anymore, so why go on a forced march down memory lane?

"True. So tell me. Why are you here?"

"Honestly?" She shook her head in wonder and admitted, "I can't believe I'm here, either. But I didn't have anywhere else to turn."

She took a small breath, covered her mouth with her fingertips and let tears well in her eyes. Something inside Rafe tightened as he remembered all the times Leslie had been able to turn on the tears. During an argument, to avoid an argument or just to make the point that he was a selfish bastard—out came the tears. When they were dating, he'd felt almost heroic when he could make those tears stop. Because she looked so damn fragile when she cried. Today though, he was no longer moved. Besides, she had a different husband now. Why wasn't she home turning *him* inside out?

"Oh, Rafe," she whispered brokenly, allowing the sunlight to backlight her to perfection. "I hated coming here, truly, but I had no choice."

"Just tell me what's going on."

"It's John," she said and Rafe felt an instant stab of

worry. After all, before he became Leslie's husband, John Peters had been Rafe's best friend.

"Is he all right?"

"Physically, yes," she said with a little shake of her head. "But Rafe, he's lost his job and I don't know what to do."

For one very brief second, Rafe felt a twinge of sympathy for his old friend. He and John had met in college and until Leslie had come between them, they'd been the best of friends. Truthfully, Rafe had missed John's friendship more than he had missed being with Leslie.

A sad statement on a dead marriage.

"What's that got to do with me?" He winced at the tone in his own voice and knew that he'd sounded crueler than he'd intended when her head came up and her eyes narrowed.

"You don't have to be mean."

He sighed and glanced at his watch. He wanted to take a shower, get dressed and pick up Katie. Leslie was his past and his present was looking a lot more promising. So rather than prolonging this conversation, he got to the point. "Leslie, you're my *ex*-wife married to my *ex*-friend. Just how much sympathy do you expect?"

"I knew you wouldn't understand."

"You're right," he agreed, heading for the wet bar along the wall. He suddenly wanted a beer. "I don't."

She walked over to join him and asked for a glass of wine. Once he'd poured it and handed it to her, Leslie took a sip and said, "I need money."

Rafe almost smiled, even as he felt a brand-new sheen of ice coat his heart. He should have known. When it came right down to it, what people wanted from the

Kings was money. Never failed. "Does John know you're here?"

"Of course not. He'd be humiliated."

That much Rafe believed. The man Rafe remembered would have been horrified to know that Leslie was here asking for help. He leaned one arm on the bar top. "Just out of curiosity, say I give you the cash you need, how do you explain that to John?"

"I'll find a way," she said, lifting her chin slightly to prove her point. "I can be pretty persuasive."

"I remember." He remembered a lot, Rafe thought. Leslie had always been able to find a way to get whatever it was she wanted. That much, it seemed, hadn't changed. As he looked at his ex-wife now, he mentally compared her to Katie Charles. Katie with her soft hair and faded jeans. With the laugh that seemed to bubble up from her soul. With green eyes that flashed from humor to fury and back again in a heartbeat.

Leslie was coolly elegant.

Katie was heat and passion and—he shut his brain off before it went on an even wilder tangent.

"Rafe, I wouldn't have come to you if I'd had anywhere else to turn," she said, and for the first time, her voice held an edge of regret.

"Yeah, I know that, too." Rafe thought about Katie again and wondered what she would do if she was in Leslie's position. He didn't like to think about Katie being in trouble. Didn't want to acknowledge that it bothered him more than a little to know that she wouldn't turn to him.

Then he thought about how hard Katie worked at building her business. How she scrambled for a living. How she worked and fought for a future doing something she loved. She would do whatever she had to do to take care of herself. And he realized that Leslie was only doing the same thing now. She never would have come to him for help if she hadn't been desperate. Hell, he could read that much in her tear-sheened blue eyes. Because of Katie, Rafe felt a surge of sympathy for Leslie he might not have experienced just a few weeks ago. What was that about?

However it had ended between them, Rafe knew he couldn't ignore Leslie's request for help. Maybe he was finally letting the past go—along with the regrets and the stinging sense of failure memories of his marriage inevitably dredged up.

"Call my assistant Janice tomorrow," he told her. "She'll give you however much you need."

She let out a relieved breath and gave him a grateful smile. "Thanks. To tell the truth, I didn't really think you'd help."

"But you asked anyway."

"Had to," she said, her gaze steady and honest. "I can't stand seeing John worried and upset."

Rafe studied her. "You really love him."

"I really do," she said simply.

That should at least sting, he thought, but it didn't. Not anymore. And, if he was honest with himself, Rafe could admit that when Leslie had walked out, it had been his pride, more than his heart, that had been affected. What did that say about him? Was Leslie right when she told him that he simply wasn't capable of love?

"Les, when we were married," he asked quietly, studying the label on his beer bottle as if looking for the right words, "did you feel that way about me? Would you have protected me if I needed it?"

"You didn't need me, Rafe," she said softly. "You never really did."

"I loved you."

She smiled and shook her head. "No, you didn't."

Irritation spiked. "I guess I know what I felt."

"Don't be so insulted," she said, giving him a patient smile. "I know you cared, but you didn't *love* me, Rafe. I finally got tired of trying to get through to you."

He straightened up, set his beer down and stuffed both hands into his jeans pockets. "I seem to recall you telling me I was incapable of love."

She blinked at him, stunned. "No, I didn't."

"Yeah, you did," he argued.

"For heaven's sake, Rafe," she countered, "why would I say that?"

"Funny, I asked myself that a few times."

"Honestly, Rafe, this is one of the reasons we didn't work out," she told him with a shake of her head. "You never *listened* to me. I never said you were *incapable* of love. I said you were incapable of loving *me*."

He shifted his gaze from Leslie to the view beyond his windows. The sun was sliding into the ocean, dazzling the waves in a brilliant crimson light. A cool breeze danced in through the open balcony doors and he turned his face into it. "Either way, you were right."

"No," Leslie said. "I wasn't."

She reached out and laid one hand on his arm. "Rafe, don't you get it? You didn't love me and that hurt. So I wanted to hurt you back."

She hadn't hurt him, he realized now. She had just driven home the point he'd learned long before her. That love was something you had to be taught when you were growing up. And that was one course Rafe had never gotten.

Leslie tipped her head to one side and looked up at him. "Who is she?"

"What?" He stiffened, instantly retreating into privacy mode, shuttering his eyes, closing down his expression. He took a long, metaphorical step back and distanced himself as much as possible from the curiosity in Leslie's eyes.

"Wow," she murmured, staring at him as if he'd just performed a magic trick, "you still do that so easily."

"Do what?"

"Lock yourself away the instant anybody gets close. Used to make me crazy," she admitted. "It was as if you were on a constant red alert—just waiting for a sneak attack on your heart so you could defend against it."

He resented the description, but Rafe really couldn't deny it, either.

Shaking her head again, she said, "Don't do it, Rafe. I mean, with her, whoever she is, don't do this. Let her in. Risk it."

"Yeah, because my track record is so good."

"You don't need a track record to love someone," she told him. "All it takes is the *right* someone."

"Like John?" he asked.

"For me, yes. Exactly like John." She let her hand fall from his arm and added, "You know, John misses your friendship. You didn't have to cut him loose because of what happened between us, Rafe."

Yes, he did. Because he couldn't look at his friend without knowing that somehow, John had been able to do something Rafe had failed at. He'd made Leslie happy when Rafe couldn't. Kings didn't like losing, probably because they weren't very good at it. Thankfully, the Kings didn't have to deal with that situation often, since they rarely accepted failure.

But in these last few minutes with Leslie, Rafe could admit that whatever he had once felt at losing her was now gone. She was married, happy and a mother. Leslie had moved on, just as his brothers had said. Maybe it was time he did the same thing. Should he really allow one failure to dictate the rest of his life?

"I've missed John, too," he admitted finally. And since that statement didn't leave a bitter taste in his mouth, he heard himself ask, "How are the kids?"

Her face brightened instantly and her smile went wide and heartfelt. "They're terrific. Want to see some pictures?"

"Sure." It only took her a moment to get her purse and pull out her wallet. Then she was flipping through pictures of two beautiful kids, each of them with her hair and John's eyes. He looked at those shining faces and felt the slightest ping of envy at the proof of his ex-wife's current life.

"Nice-looking kids."

"They're great," Leslie said. "And John's a wonderful father."

"I'm glad for you," he told her and surprisingly enough, he meant it. Odd, Rafe thought. Before, when he'd thought about Leslie, there had always been a thread of sadness sliding through him. His failure. His mistake. Now, he felt nothing like that. Instead, his thoughts were filled with images of Katie Charles. Her smile. Her laugh. The feel of her skin beneath his hands.

Leslie was the past.

Was Katie the future?

"Are you okay?"

"What?"

Leslie studied him. "You looked worried there for a second."

Worried? Him? Rafe frowned slightly. He didn't

worry. He acted. "No. Not worried. Everything's fine." He paused and then surprised himself by adding, "I'm glad you stopped by today, Leslie."

"Yeah?" She grinned. "Now there's something you wouldn't have said even a year ago."

"True," he admitted ruefully. "But I can say it now."

"She must really be something, your mystery woman."

"You know," he said thoughtfully, as the last of his baggage from his failed marriage fell away, "she really is."

"Then don't blow it, Rafe," Leslie told him. "For your own sake, let her in."

He already had, he realized now. Hadn't meant to. Hadn't even been aware of it. But somehow Katie had gotten past his defenses and now he had to figure out what that meant for him. For them.

"I should be going," Leslie said. She picked up her bag and walked over to slip into her heels. "Thank you again for doing this, Rafe, and I will pay you back."

"I know. Just…call Janice tomorrow."

"I will. Oh, and don't be mad at Declan for letting me into your place. I won't do it again."

He nodded, watching her prepare to return to her own life and world.

"There's one more thing," she said softly. "I'm sorry about how we ended."

He snapped her a look and noted that her smile was genuine and the tears were gone. For the first time, Rafe could look at her and see beyond his own failures and disappointments. He realized that there weren't hard feelings anymore. He didn't need to continue to avoid Leslie or even John. The past was done. It didn't matter to him now and with that realization came a sort of peace. So when another thought popped into his mind, he went with it.

"We could always use another legal shark at King Construction," he offered. "Tell John to call me."

Her smile was quick and bright. "He'd love to talk to you again, Rafe. Even without a job offer."

"Yeah," he admitted. "Me, too."

When Leslie left a moment later, Rafe took a second or two to enjoy the unusual sensation he felt. For years, he'd been holding on to the failure of his marriage like a damn battle flag. Internally, he'd waved it any time a woman even remotely seemed to be getting too close. That stamp of failure was enough to ensure he'd never try marriage again. Never allow someone to matter too much. As a King, he didn't fail.

But now, he was beginning to realize that maybe his marriage to Leslie hadn't had a chance from the beginning. He'd never had a shot at making it work because he had married Leslie for all the wrong reasons.

They had both been too young to know what they wanted. Too stupid to see that getting married wasn't the natural end result of dating for a year. He had blindly pushed forward even though a part of him had known going in that it wasn't right.

The problem was, he didn't feel like that about Katie. Being with her felt absolutely right. But would it still feel that way when she knew the truth?

Nine

After a long nap, Katie felt energized and a little nervous about her upcoming date. So she took moral support along when she went shopping.

"Seriously?" Nicole asked, shaking her head and grimacing. "You're not fifty years old, Katie."

Katie looked down at the dress she had tried on and frowned to herself. It was a lovely beige silk with a high neck, long sleeves and a full skirt that swirled around her knees when she did a quick turn in front of the mirror. "It's pretty."

"It's dowdy," Nicole argued and handed Connor a bottle of juice.

The little boy kicked his heels against the stroller bottom and cried out, "Pretty!"

"Connor likes it," Katie argued.

"He won't when he's thirty." Nicole shook her head again, leaned over to a nearby rack and plucked a dress free. "Try this one. It's your size."

"It's black."

"And…?"

Katie blew out a breath and said, "Fine. Be right back."

They were in a tiny boutique on Second Street. She might have had better luck in a mall, but this was closer and Katie preferred supporting the small businesses around her. After all, she was determined to be one of them someday soon and besides, the big mega stores already had a huge customer base.

She took off the beige and hung it up carefully, giving it one last wistful glance. "Are you sure?" she called out from the dressing room. "The beige one looks so elegant."

"Try the black," Nicole ordered from just outside the door. "Trust me on this."

Sighing, Katie did, dragging the black dress over her head and positioning it just right. When she closed the side zipper, she looked into the mirror and instantly thought about buying a sweater.

"I can't wear this," she complained, still staring at her reflection as if seeing a stranger. "This is so not me."

"Let's see it."

Katie opened the door a scant inch, barely giving Nicole a peek. But her friend wasn't satisfied with that and pushed the door open completely. Her eyes went wide and a slow grin curved her mouth. "Wow."

Uncomfortable, Katie looked back into the mirror. Miles of skin were exposed. She'd never worn anything like this before. And what did that say about her sad, quiet little life?

Two thin black straps snaked over her bare shoulders and the bodice was cut low enough to give an excellent view of the tops of her breasts. The material was slick and clingy and molded to every inch of her body, defining curves even she hadn't been aware of. The hem of the dress hit mid-thigh—another inch or two higher and it would've been illegal.

As it was, it was only embarrassing.

"You look amazing," Nicole said, staring into the mirror to catch her eye.

"I can't wear this."

"Why not?"

"It's just not me," Katie said, fighting the urge to tug the bodice up a little higher.

"That's exactly why you should wear it," Nicole told her, scooping Connor out of the stroller to prop him on her hip. Swinging her blond hair back behind her shoulder, she met Katie's gaze in the mirror and said, "Cordell shot your confidence out from under you."

"True." But she was the one who had allowed it to happen. Katie ran one hand over the front of the dress, smoothing the fabric. She studied her own reflection while her friend continued talking.

"If you keep hiding away, you're letting *him* decide your life for you. Don't you get it?"

Katie's gaze shifted to Nicole's in the mirror. "Yes, but—"

"No buts." Nicole shook her head firmly and ran the palm of her hand across the top of her son's head. "Trust me, I know what it's like to have your self-assurance shaken. Let's pause to remember that my husband walked out on me when I was pregnant."

"Nicole…"

"Not a bid for sympathy," she said firmly. "I'm so over him. My point is, you should be over Cordell, too."

"I am really," Katie told her and realized that she had been "over" Cordell for some time. She'd been nursing her own hurt feelings for too long, but that had stopped when she met Rafe.

Just one of his kisses was enough to sear anyone else from her mind. Her heart. Her breath caught and twisted in her lungs until she was almost light-headed as she thought about the gleam that would appear in Rafe's eyes when he saw her in this dress.

"Then what're you waiting for?" Nicole came up behind her. In the glass, the two women stood side by side, with a toddler boy grinning between them. "If you're really over that creep, then wear this dress tonight. Knock Rafe's socks off."

Katie sent her own reflection a thoughtful smile. Slowly, she straightened up, threw her shoulders back and let the initial embarrassment she'd felt slide away. She did look good. She really liked Rafe and hiding away from what she was feeling wouldn't change that any.

"Atta girl," Nicole whispered as if she could hear what Katie was thinking.

Katie's mind raced. Cordell King hadn't even been a part of her life for very long. Truthfully, she thought now, she had probably built what they'd so briefly shared into something it had never been. Meeting him had been so far out of her orbit that she had taken it as some sort of sign—that he was the one. She had been willingly blinded by the fairy tale, Katie told herself hollowly. Rich, handsome man sweeps poor but honest shopkeeper off her feet and whisks her off to his palatial estate.

She gave her reflection a rueful smile.

When her fantasy ended, she'd crawled back into her narrow routine and pulled it in after her, essentially cutting herself off from everything just so that she couldn't make a foolish mistake again. And who was *that* decision hurting? she demanded silently.

Cordell had gone on his merry way, leaving a diamond token in his wake, no doubt never once thinking about Katie. While she, on the other hand, had not only buried herself in work, but continued to hold off on another relationship just because she'd made one bad judgment call.

Straightening up slowly, she looked her reflection in the eye and asked, *Are you going to be alone for the rest of your life, Katie?*

God no. She didn't want that. She had never wanted that. Ever since she was a little girl, she'd dreamed about having a family of her own. She had heard all the stories from her grandmother and her mother, talking about the great loves of their lives and how they wouldn't have traded a minute of it—even to spare themselves the pain of losing those special men.

What, she wondered, would she look back on one day? A great cookie recipe?

"So just when exactly did I become such a coward?" she whispered.

"What?"

She shifted her gaze to Nicole's reflection and asked, "Why didn't I see this before? Why am I hiding away? I didn't do anything wrong. I just picked a lemon in the garden of love."

Nicole laughed and the baby's giggle echoed her. "Nice way of putting it, but yeah."

Every passing moment filled Katie with more strength. More confidence. Right there in the tiny dressing room, she had the epiphany of all epiphanies. She had closed herself off to life to punish herself for being wrong. It didn't even make sense. Was pain so great that you couldn't risk being happy on the off chance you might get hurt again?

It was as if she could feel her old self clawing her way to the surface, brushing past the hesitant, meek Katie and tamping her down, she hoped, never to rise again.

"Who doesn't pick the wrong guy occasionally?" she demanded.

"Preaching to the choir, girl," Nicole said ruefully.

"That's right!" Katie swung around and draped one arm around Nicole's shoulders. "*Your* guy was a jerk, too!"

Laughing, Nicole said, "Do you have to sound so excited by that?"

Katie shook her head and said, "Sorry, but I'm having a moment here. The problem's not me. It never was me. So I picked the wrong guy? So what? Doesn't mean I'll pick the wrong one again, does it?"

"Nope."

Swinging back around to face her reflection, Katie dismissed the dowdy beige dress from her mind and instead admired the sexy black one she wore. She turned and checked herself out from every angle and finally gave a sharp nod. "You were right, Nicole. This dress *is* perfect. It's going to knock Rafe's socks off."

"Hopefully," Nicole added with a sly grin, "it'll knock off a lot more than his socks."

Katie felt a flush of heat rush through her just thinking about the possibilities. Then she tugged at the zipper and said, "As soon as I'm dressed again, we're headed for the shoe department. I need some sky-high heels, too."

"Now you're talking," Nicole said and took her son out of the dressing room.

Katie thought about what Rafe's reaction to her might be and she smiled to herself. She was through pretending she didn't care about him. Finished trying to protect herself at the cost of her own happiness. Tonight was going to be a turning point for her and Rafe. She was opening herself up to the possibilities.

Katie gave her reflection one last, approving glance. Nana would be so proud.

The restaurant sat high on the cliffs at Dana Point.

There was patio dining and then there were the booths inside, safely tucked behind a glass wall, protecting diners from the cool wind. He'd left their choice of table up to Katie and was pleased when she'd opted for the patio. From here, they could not only see the ocean, but hear the pulse of it as the water met the cliffs.

With the stars overhead and the waves crashing into the rocks below, it was probably one of the most romantic places on the coast. Rafe hadn't been there in years—but he had known it was the perfect spot for the romantic evening he wanted to have with Katie.

Looking at her now, across the table from him, with the ocean breeze ruffling her dark red hair into a tumble of curls, his breath caught in his chest. Her green eyes shone in the soft candlelight burning from behind the safety of hurricane lamps in the center of their table. Her smile was infectious as she admired her surroundings, and the urge to reach out and touch her was damn near overpowering.

He'd never forget his first sight of her when she opened her door to him. That black dress clung to her body in all the right ways. Her creamy skin was displayed to perfection and the heels she wore made her already great legs look amazing.

Everything in him went hard and tight. His heartbeat was crashing in his chest and his mind filled with sensual images of just how he hoped this evening would end.

"This place is gorgeous," she said, shifting her gaze

back to him before turning her head to take in the restaurant behind them and the people sitting behind the glass wall. "I can't believe anyone would choose to be inside instead of out here."

"Me either," he said and reached for his glass of wine. He took a sip, admired the taste of it and silently toasted his cousin Travis, who owned and operated King Vineyards. The bottle of King Cabernet was perfect. As it should be. "But most women prefer to be inside where their hair doesn't get messed up by the wind."

She turned to grin at him, flipping her hair back over her shoulder. "Not me. I love the feel of the wind."

"It looks good on you," he said softly.

Katie took a sip of her wine and smiled. "The wine's good, too, even if it *is* from the King winery."

Frowning a bit, Rafe told himself he should have ordered a different wine, if only to keep her mind off the King family and her resentments toward them. Clearly, tonight would not be the night when he'd make a full confession. He would soon, though. He just had to find the right words. The right way to explain to her who he was and why he'd lied to her.

Just as he was about to change the subject, he thought better of it and decided to plunge in and try to subtly alter her opinion of the Kings.

"They can't all be bad," he said diffidently.

"Maybe not," she allowed and he felt a small stirring of hope that was dashed a moment later. "But people that rich are so removed from everyday life they tend to look at the world differently than we do."

One of his eyebrows lifted. "You know many rich people, do you?"

She smiled. "No. Just the one. But he left an impression."

"Obviously," Rafe murmured, still wishing he knew which member of his family had hurt her so badly.

Reaching across the table, Katie covered Rafe's hand with her own and his fingers trapped hers instantly, holding on to her when she would have pulled back. She tipped her head to one side and said, "The difference between you and a rich guy is that you brought me here because you thought I'd love it. He would have brought me here to impress me. That's a big difference, Rafe."

He shifted a bit in his chair, uncomfortable with her explanation. The truth was, he'd brought her here because he *had* wanted to impress her—but he'd also known that she would love this place. So that was sort of a compromise, wasn't it?

Still holding on to her hand, he stroked the pad of his thumb across her fingers and said quietly, "What if the rich guy really did bring you here because he thought you'd like it?"

She smiled and briefly gave his hand a squeeze. "It still wouldn't have been as special as you bringing me here, because I know that for a working guy, this place is so expensive, you wouldn't come here normally."

The frown he felt earlier came back as he studied her. "You know something? You're a snob, Katie Charles."

"What?" She tugged her hand free and sat up straight in her chair. "No, I'm not."

"Sure you are," he countered, suddenly feeling more relaxed. If he could make her see that she was being prejudiced, maybe she'd take the truth, when he finally told it, a little better. "On the strength of meeting one rich creep, you've decided that all rich guys aren't worth your time. So you're a reverse snob. As far as you're concerned, only poor guys need apply."

"That sounds terrible," she said, reaching for her wine. She took a sip and set the glass down again.

"But it's accurate." Rafe grinned, and took her hand in his again, despite her efforts to wriggle free.

"Nice to know what you really think of me."

"What I think is, you're a beautiful, smart, ambitious woman with one huge blind spot."

She laughed in spite of herself. "That's a heck of a description."

"This guy who treated you so badly," Rafe said, ignoring her last comment. "What was it about him that attracted you in the first place?"

Her mouth twisted a little and she took a breath, then blew it out in a huff. "Fine. I admit it. He was…" She lifted one shoulder in a half shrug. "…exciting. Different. He was rich and handsome and—"

"Hmm," Rafe teased in a thoughtful tone. She'd said exactly what he'd hoped she would say. Made it much easier to score a point here. "So the first thing you noticed about him was that he was rich?"

"Not the first," she argued quickly, then after a second or two she admitted, "but it was in the top two."

"Uh-huh."

"Fine. I see what you're saying." She shook her wind-tousled hair back from her face. "Very clever. So the poor rich man was taken advantage of by a woman who was intrigued."

"Nope, not what I'm saying at all," he told her, keeping her hand firmly in his despite the fact that she kept trying to slip free. "All I'm saying is that you liked that he was rich until it turned on you. So basically, the problem here is that he was a jerk, not that he was a *rich* jerk."

Whatever she might have said in response went

unspoken because their server chose that moment to arrive with their salads. Rafe and Katie stared into each others' eyes as the woman deftly slid icy plates in front of them and asked, "Is there anything else you need right now?"

"No, thanks." Rafe dismissed her with a smile, then turned his gaze back on Katie, who was watching him through narrowed eyes.

"Think you're pretty clever, don't you?" she asked.

"Actually, *yeah.*"

She laughed and the sound of it was like music to him.

"Okay, I see your point," she acknowledged, picking up her fork. "And maybe you're a little bit right."

"Only a little?" he asked.

"Yes," she said. "I didn't like him *because* he was rich, but I do admit that was part of the attraction. Mainly since I couldn't understand why he was interested in me."

"I can."

Rafe understood completely what any man would see in Katie. What he couldn't understand was how a member of his family could be so stupid as to walk away from her. To hurt her and toss her aside. That he would never figure out. But if his anonymous relative hadn't walked away from Katie, Rafe wouldn't be with her now. So maybe he owed the bastard a thank-you—after he punched him in the face.

She smiled. "Thanks for that. And I'll think about what you said. Maybe you're right. Maybe it's not rich guys I should be mad at, but the jerks of the world."

He lifted his glass in a silent toast to her, even while thinking that if she was going to condemn the "jerks," wouldn't he technically be one of that crowd? The burden of lies fell on top of him and Rafe couldn't shrug it off anymore. He wasn't looking forward to telling her the truth, but he couldn't see a way around it.

"Deal." He reluctantly released her hand so that she could eat her salad, but he found he missed the warmth of her touch. He watched her in the flickering candlelight and though the restaurant patio was crowded with other diners, it felt to him as though he and Katie were all alone.

He didn't need dinner. Didn't need the wine. All he really needed—*wanted*—was this woman sitting across from him. She was unlike anyone he'd ever known. She didn't want anything from him. Didn't demand his attention—though she had it anyway. In another week or so, her kitchen redo would be complete and he wouldn't have a handy excuse for seeing her every day. That thought settled like a black cloud over his heart and it was just another reminder that he didn't want to let her go.

He wasn't sure if that meant they had a future or not, but what it did mean was he wanted her for more than a few stolen moments.

This had never been about a future with Katie, he reminded himself. This had started out as a way to reclaim the King family reputation. But there was more to it than that now. He had planned to simply woo her, win her and then move on. Go back to his life and leave Katie to hers.

But since that plan wasn't as appealing as it had been before, he clearly needed a new plan.

He only wished he knew what that was.

Ten

Two hours later, dinner was over and instead of taking her home, Rafe helped Katie down to the beach.

"These heels are *not* made for walking in the sand," she said with a laugh. She stopped and pulled off first one shoe then the other and looked up at him with a grin. "There. That's better."

High above them, diners still filled the restaurant patio. But here on the moonlit beach, they were alone in the shadows, as if they were the only two people on the coast. And Rafe couldn't take his eyes off her. She was the most captivating woman he'd ever known. She thought nothing of kicking off her heels to take a walk on the beach with him. She didn't worry about her hair and she didn't whine about being cold. She was... amazing and he felt a hard, solid punch of something he couldn't identify somewhere around his heart.

She laid one hand on his chest. "Rafe? You okay?"

"Yeah," he told her, "I'm fine."

But he wasn't at all sure. Leading her along the beach, Rafe held her hand and made sure she didn't get wet as the tide rushed in, leaving a foaming layer of lace on the sand. The coast was dark, but the ocean shone with moonlight glittering on its surface.

"Tonight was perfect," she said and leaned her head on his shoulder. "But you didn't have to take me to such an expensive restaurant."

He dropped her hand and laid one arm around her shoulders. "You didn't like it?"

"I loved it," she admitted. "I just don't want you to think you have to spend a lot of money to impress me."

There was a first, he told himself wryly. He couldn't remember anyone ever telling him not to spend money on them. Hell, his own mother only came around when her bank account was empty. And even thinking that made him feel like a child demanding something he couldn't have. Ridiculous. He didn't *need* anybody. He was better alone. At least he always had been. Now, he wasn't so sure. His mind was racing with thoughts that contradicted each other. Back away, one side of him said. Have a few great nights with Katie, then tell her the truth and leave her behind. But there was another voice in his mind now, too. And it was saying something completely different. That maybe Katie was what had been missing from his life. That maybe, if he could find a way to dig himself out of the hole he found himself in, he might actually find *love*.

That thought was both intriguing and terrifying to a man with so little experience with love.

She threaded her arm through his and snuggled closer and his heartbeat quickened even as his brain raced. Damn, what was going on with him? All his body wanted to do was slow down, enjoy her. Hold her. But his mind wouldn't let him relax into the moment. It kept insisting that Katie was different. Special. That she deserved honesty, damn it. That he was risking something potentially wonderful by lying to her.

"What're you thinking about?" she asked, coming to a stop so she could tip her head back to look up at him.

"You," he said.

She reached up and smoothed his hair back from his forehead and the touch of her fingers sent heat jolting through him.

"They don't look like happy thoughts. Should I be worried?"

"No," he said quickly. He threaded his fingers through her hair and she turned her face into his palm. "Did I tell you how beautiful you are?"

"Yeah, I think you mentioned it a time or two."

"Well, since I don't like repeating myself, why don't I show you instead?"

He kissed her thoroughly, completely, parting her lips with his tongue and sweeping into the warmth he'd found only with her. She welcomed him, leaning into his embrace, matching his desire with her own. He held her tightly to him, drawing her as close as possible and still it wasn't enough.

Here on this lonely stretch of beach, with the moonlight spilling down on them, Rafe could only think of her. Nothing else mattered. Only the next kiss and the next. Touching her, being with her. His brain was finally silenced by his body's overwhelming need.

He swept one hand along her side, feeling the curves of her through the silky coolness of her dress. He cupped her breast and she arched into him, a soft moan issuing from her throat. His thumb stroked the peak of her rigid nipple and even through the fabric separating him from her, he could feel her heat reaching for him.

Not enough, he thought wildly. Not nearly enough. He needed to feel her skin. Flesh to flesh. Heat to heat. He shifted her in his arms and while his mouth tantalized hers, his hand swept to the hem of her dress and inched it up, higher and higher. His palm moved over her thigh, sliding toward her core, and she parted her legs for him.

That first touch inflamed him, though the silk of her panties kept him from delving as deeply as he wanted— needed—to. He stroked her center and she shivered, that soft moan erupting over and over again as he brushed his fingertips over her most sensitive flesh.

The sea wind caressed them, the moonlight coated them in a silvery light and all Rafe was aware of was the woman in his arms. The woman he wanted above all things. He pushed the edge of her panties to one side, stroked that one tender spot at the heart of her and felt her tremble in his arms, quaking and shivering. Again and again, he touched her, pushing her higher, faster. He dipped his fingers deep, stroking her, inside and out. Her legs parted farther as she plastered herself against him. Rafe's tongue twisted with hers, he took her breath, each labored gasp, as she twisted and writhed against him, hungry for the climax shuddering just out of reach.

He reveled in her response. Loved knowing that she was as hungry for him as he was for her. He continued to push her, using his hand, his fingers, to urge her toward completion, needing to feel her surrender.

Then it was there, a release crashing down over her with enough force to leave them both shaken.

Her hands clutched at his shoulders, and her hips rocked into his hand, riding him as he took her quickly, inexorably into a shower of stars.

When it was done, when she hung limp in his arms, he tore his mouth from hers. It nearly killed him to stop, but he gathered his strength and rested his forehead against hers, each of them struggling for breath that wouldn't come. After several long seconds, he smoothed her skirt back down and whispered, "Let's go back to your place."

"Yes," she said, her voice husky with satisfaction and growing need. "Let's go now."

He grinned at her, swept her up into his arms and carried her back across the beach to the cement stairs leading up to Pacific Coast Highway.

Laughing, she said, "Rafe, I can walk, you know."

He brushed a quick kiss across her mouth. "Yeah, but I really liked carrying you before. Thought it was worth repeating."

At the head of the stairs, he took a left and made for the restaurant. He was suddenly grateful he hadn't used valet parking. They wouldn't have to stand around and wait for the car to be brought up. Instead, he'd make a dash to the lot and swing back around to pick her up.

Kissing her again, he dropped her to her feet, cupped her face in his palms and said, "Wait here. I'll get the car."

"I can come with you."

"Faster if I run for it and those heels aren't made for running."

"True," she said, glancing down at the sexy black heels she'd stepped into again the moment they were off the beach. "Hurry up."

"Back in a flash," he promised and raced off into the parking lot.

Katie watched him go, her gaze locked on him until he was swallowed up by the crowd of cars and the hazy light thrown from the yellow fog lamps. Her heart was pounding and every inch of her body was tingling, throbbing still from the effects of the orgasm still rattling through her.

The ocean wind was cold now, but it couldn't even touch the heat flooding her body. She smiled to herself, thinking that the splurge on the dress and shoes had been totally worth it. Having him touch her, take her, on the beach beneath the moon had been an experience she would never forget. The man was far too sexy for his own good and his touch was magic.

The whole night had been perfect and was, she told herself with another smile, about to get even better.

She was going to be happy, damn it. She wasn't going to deprive herself of the chance to be with Rafe because of old fears and trust issues. She wouldn't pass up a shot at happiness because of past mistakes. Besides, she had been thinking about what Rafe had said earlier all night.

He had a point. Part of what had attracted her to Cordell had been the fact that he was rich. So what did that say about her? She couldn't really blame his actions on the fact that he had money any more than she could blame her response on the fact that she *wasn't* wealthy.

They were just people.

And people made mistakes, right? The important thing was to learn from them and try not to make the *same* mistakes over and over again.

She remembered the feel of Rafe's arms coming

around her. The slow, intimate caresses. The heat of desire and the warmth of love rushing between them and her breath caught in her chest. She hadn't realized it until just this moment, and now that she had, she couldn't imagine how it had escaped her for this long.

Katie was in love.

Real love. She knew the difference this time and she wrapped herself up in the amazing sensations as they spiraled through her. What she'd thought she felt for Cordell before wasn't even a glimmer of what she felt for Rafe now. He was everything she had hoped to find. He was the man she had been waiting for all of her life.

How had it happened so quickly?

But even as she wondered that, she smiled to herself, remembering that Nana had always said "Love doesn't go by the clock." One moment was all it took when it was real. One amazing moment when the world suddenly became clear and your heart knew exactly what it wanted and needed.

She sighed a little and held her newfound knowledge close. Tonight was a night she would remember forever.

"Katie?" A deep voice called her name. "Katie Charles? Is that you?"

A small thread of something unpleasant unwound throughout her system as Katie turned slowly toward that too-familiar voice. She saw him instantly, but then he was hard to miss. Tall, gorgeous, black hair long enough to lay on his collar and sharp blue eyes fixed on her.

Cordell King.

She stood her ground and lifted her chin as he walked to her. She shouldn't have been surprised to see him.

She knew he lived in Laguna Beach and this restaurant, being the most expensive one in miles, would surely be a draw to him. But what did amaze her was the fact that she felt *nothing* for him. There were no leftover feelings trapped inside her. Not even anger, though as he smiled at her as if they were long lost friends, she could feel a spark of irritation flash into life.

"It's great to see you," Cordell said as he got close enough. He swept her into a brief hug whether she wanted to go or not, then released her. "You look amazing."

"Thanks," she said, even more grateful now that she'd bought the fabulous black dress. Imagine if she'd run into him wearing that beige one.

He glanced around, then asked, "Are you here alone? Can I buy you a drink?"

"No, you can't," she said, amazed that he had even asked. "I'm sure the woman you're with wouldn't appreciate the company."

"No date," he said. "I'm here meeting a couple of my brothers."

"Well, I'm here with someone else. He's just gone to get the car."

"Oh." He shrugged and gave her that slow, easy smile that had first tugged at her. "Well, not surprising you've got a date. You look great."

"You said that already."

"Yeah, I know," he told her. That smile came back, but when she didn't respond, he continued. "Look, Katie. I'm actually glad we ran into each other. I've been doing a lot of thinking about you lately."

Now that was surprising. "Is that right?"

"Yeah," he said, stepping in a little closer. "I was

going to call you, but doing this in person is even better."

"Why's that?" she asked sharply, folding her arms over her chest. "You didn't think breaking up with me was important enough to do in person. You overnighted me a diamond bracelet along with that charming note that said something along the lines of 'Our worlds are just too different.' Remember?"

He had the good grace to wince at the reminder, but it wasn't enough to shut him down completely. *Oh, no, not a King,* she thought.

"Okay, I could've handled that better," he acknowledged. "But I did send you diamonds."

And she'd sold them to help pay for the kitchen remodel, Katie told herself.

"I never asked for diamonds," she pointed out.

"No, but—" He stopped, took a breath and said, "Look, we're getting off the subject."

"Which is?" The toe of her shoe tapped against the cement, making a staccato sound that played counterpoint to the conversation.

"I'd like to give our relationship another chance," he said. "I mean, we had a great time for a while—"

"Until you dumped me, you mean?" she interrupted, that spark of irritation flashing into quite the little blaze.

"Yeah, well." He shrugged as if that were water under the bridge. "That was then, this is now. And, babe, looking at you now makes me think we could work things out if we tried."

"Babe?" she repeated, taking one step toward him. "Don't you call me 'babe.'"

"Hey." He lifted both hands in the air as if he were

surrendering, but that meant nothing. "Relax, I just thought—"

"You just thought that I'd what? Leap into your arms at the *gracious* offer of being able to go out with you again?"

He smiled and that simply infuriated her. Cordell King had bruised her heart so badly, she'd completely lost sight of who and what she was. He'd shattered her confidence and made her question her own ability to judge a person's character.

"All I'm saying is—" he started.

But Katie cut him off with a single wave of her hand. She was through. She didn't want to hear his lame excuses. He'd hurt her and now he behaved as though it had never happened. Well, maybe most of the Kings were able to skate through life without ever once having to face up to what they'd done, but Cordell was going to get a piece of her mind. At last.

"Don't bother. I'm not interested in what you have to say. Do you really think I would go out with you again after how you treated me? Seriously? Does that sweet smile and charm really work for you?"

"Usually," he admitted, taking a long step back as if finally understanding that she wasn't thrilled to see him. He took a quick look around as if to assure himself that they were alone.

They were. But it wouldn't have mattered to Katie either way.

"Amazing," she said, "that there are so many women out there allowing themselves to be dazzled by good looks and empty promises."

"Now just a minute," he countered in his own defense. "I didn't make you any promises."

"Oh, no," she acknowledged. "Just the unspoken

promise of one human being to treat another with a bit of respect."

"It was a good time, okay? That's all. As for tonight, I saw you and thought—"

"I know exactly what you thought, Cordell, and I can tell you it's never going to happen."

He shook his head, blew out a breath and said, "Okay, I can see that this was a mistake, so—"

The sound of a rumbling engine came to her and Katie glanced at the parking lot. Rafe was driving his truck around to the front to pick her up and as he approached, she pointed at him.

"You see that truck? Driving it is a better man than you'll ever be, Cordell. He's a carpenter. He's not rich, but he's got more class than you could hope to have. He's honest and kind and sweet and—"

"Okay!" Cordell took another step away from her and his features clearly said that he wished he were anywhere but there. "I get the picture."

"Good." She set her hands at her hips and took a deep, calming breath of the cool, fresh air. Katie felt better than she had in months. Being given the chance to face Cordell and tell him exactly what she thought of him had been…liberating.

She was still watching him with a gleam of triumph in her eyes when she heard the truck stop and the driver's side door open and slam shut.

"Cordell?" Rafe shouted as he came closer.

Katie slowly swiveled her head to stare at him. How did he know Cordell?

"Rafe?" Cordell said his name on a laugh. "*You're* the poor but honest carpenter? The paragon of virtue Katie just slapped me upside the head with? *You?*"

Rafe didn't say another word. He bunched his fist

and threw a punch to Cordell's jaw that had the man sprawled out on the cement before he could take his next breath. Then Rafe stood over him, glaring in fury. "You son of a bitch."

"You *know* each other?" Katie asked, her voice hitching higher on every word.

Rubbing his jaw, Cordell scrambled to his feet, his glare burning into Rafe as if he could set fire to him with only the power of his will. "You could say that. Rafe's my cousin."

Katie staggered back a step or two, her gaze locked on the man turning to face her now. "Rafe *King?*"

"I can explain," he said.

She noticed he wasn't denying it.

"So much for the poor but proud carpenter, huh?" Cordell muttered, his gaze snapping from his cousin to the woman staring at both of them as if they'd just crawled out from under the same rock. "Katie, I admit it. I treated you badly and I'm sorry for it. But at least I never lied to you, which is more than I can say for my cousin."

"Shut up, Cordell."

"You want to try another shot at me, Rafe?" he offered. "Go for it."

"Both of you stop it," Katie demanded, suddenly feeling like a bone being tugged between two snarling dogs.

Fury tangled with hurt and mixed into a knot of emotions in the pit of her stomach. She was so shaken she could hardly stand, but still, she had to look at Rafe. She read regret in his eyes, though that didn't do a thing toward assuaging what she was going through.

Tears stung her eyes, but she refused to let them fall. Damned if she'd give her tears to the Kings. Again. No, instead, she went with the fury, letting her anger pulse inside her until she could hardly breathe for the fire churning inside her.

"Was this a game?" she demanded, ignoring Cordell, giving her attention only to the man she had thought she knew so well. "Did you have a good time? Are you going to run off to your country club now with lots of fun stories about how you wormed your way into the cookie queen's bed?"

"You slept with her?" Cordell said.

Rafe sent him a death glare, then focused on Katie. "It wasn't a game. Damn it, Katie, you're...*important* to me."

"Oh, sure," she said, sarcasm dripping from her tone, "I can sense that. Lies are always an indicator of a real depth of feeling."

"I was going to tell you the truth."

"What stopped you?" she asked tightly. "Could it be shame?"

"Katie, if you'll just listen for a second..." He took a step closer and she skipped back in reaction.

"Stay away from me," she muttered, shaking her head as if she could wipe away the memory of these last few minutes. "I can't believe this is happening."

"Katie let me explain," Rafe said.

"This should be good," Cordell murmured.

"Don't you have somewhere to go?" Rafe challenged.

"I'm not going anywhere," his cousin said.

"Then I will," Katie told both of them. She couldn't stand here listening to either one of them.

"Not before you hear me out," Rafe said, grabbing her arm to hold her still when she would have sailed past him.

Katie pulled free, ignoring the instinct to stay within the grip of his warmth. "Fine. Talk."

He shot another look at his cousin, then focused on her as if she were the only person in the world. "I made a bet with Joe. The contractor."

"A *bet?* You bet on me?" Oh, she thought grimly, this just got better and better. Now it wasn't just Rafe lying to her, but Joe, too. And probably Steve and Arturo, as well. They must have had some fun lunchtime conversations talking about how stupid she was. "I can't believe you did that."

"No," he snapped, then ran one hand through his hair. "It wasn't about you. I lost a bet and had to work a job site. Your job site. Then I met you and found out you hated all the Kings because of what this moron did to you—"

"Hey!"

"—so I didn't tell you who I was. I wanted you to get to know me. To like me. Then I was going to tell you the truth, I swear it."

"*That* was your plan?" Cordell asked. "And you call me a moron."

"Be quiet, Cordell." Katie shook her head in disbelief and gave her full attention to Rafe again. His eyes were flashing with emotion, but she couldn't read them and wouldn't have bothered if she could. She was beyond caring what he was feeling. Her own emotions were too wild. Too tangled and twisted to be able to make sense of them. All she knew was that she was hurting and, once again, a *King* was at the center of her pain. "You were going to show me that I was wrong about your family by *lying* to me?"

He scrubbed one hand across his jaw and muttered

something she didn't quite catch. Then he said, "Katie, let me take you home so we can talk this out."

Cordell snorted a short laugh.

Neither of them so much as glanced at him.

"I'm not going anywhere with you, Rafe," she said quietly. Looking up into his beautiful blue eyes for the last time, she silently said goodbye to her hopes, her dreams and the love she had so recently discovered. How could she love a man she didn't even know? And that knowledge made the pain in her heart much more fierce. "Just leave me alone."

She started walking and only paused when he called out, "You need a ride home."

"I'll call a cab," she said without even looking at him.

Katie couldn't bear it for another minute. Couldn't look at him one more time, knowing that he'd lied to her every day they were together. None of it had been real. None of it had meant a thing.

She had fallen in love with a stranger.

And now she was alone again.

As the restaurant valet called for a taxi, she realized that she had been right earlier.

Tonight *was* a night she would always remember.

"So," Cordell asked, "you want to get a drink?"

"Sure," Rafe grumbled, "why not?"

The two cousins headed for the restaurant bar and Rafe didn't miss the fact that Katie's gaze locked on them both as they walked past her. He could almost feel the fury radiating off her and damned if he could blame her for it.

Amazing, he thought, just how fast a perfect night

could go to hell. As they stepped into the restaurant, Cordell shivered.

"Did you feel those icicles she was shooting at us?"

"Felt more like knives to me," Rafe said and led the way into the wood-paneled bar. A dozen or more people were scattered around the glass-walled room at tiny round tables boasting flickering candlelight. Rafe ignored everyone else and headed directly for the bartender. He took a seat, ordered two beers, then turned to look at his cousin as Cordell took the stool beside him. "This wasn't how I saw tonight ending up."

"Guess not," Cordell said amiably. "So how long have you been seeing Katie?"

"A few weeks." Rafe picked up his beer and took a long swallow.

"A few weeks? Hell, I dated her for three months and never got past her front door."

Rafe smiled to himself. That was good to hear. If Cordell had said something about sleeping with Katie, then Rafe would have had to kill him and there would have been hell to pay from the rest of the family.

As it was, he was fighting down an urge to hit Cordell again just for the heck of it. But what would be the point? Katie had made it all too clear that it wasn't just Cordell she was angry at anymore. Seemed there was plenty of outraged fury to spread over the whole King family.

And he'd brought it all on himself.

Rafe rubbed the back of his neck and gritted his teeth against the urge to howl in frustration. Ironic that just when he'd decided to come clean and confess all, he'd lost everything before he had the chance. He should have told her sooner, he knew. But he hadn't wanted to risk what they had.

Now, it no longer mattered because what they had was gone.

His cousin nudged him with an elbow. "So why'd you lie to Katie?"

"Why were you a jerk to her?"

Cordell shrugged. "According to most of the women I go out with, that's what I'm best at."

"That's just great," Rafe said, nodding grimly.

"You're avoiding the question," his cousin said. "Why'd you lie to Katie?"

"You heard me explain it to her," Rafe said, studying his own sorry reflection in the mirror across from him.

"Yeah," Cordell agreed. "But I'm thinking it was more than that."

Listening to his cousin was making Rafe bunch his fists again. He didn't want to be here with Cordell. He wanted to be with Katie. Wanted to make her understand…*what?* What could he possibly say now that wouldn't paint him as the same kind of ass as Cordell?

She had lumped all the Kings into one bad basket and as it turned out, he told himself, she was right.

"What're you talking about, Cordell?"

"Only that you really liked her. And once you found out she hated all Kings—"

"Thanks to you," Rafe added.

Cordell shrugged and nodded. "Thanks to me, then you decided that you didn't want to blow it by telling her the truth."

"Wrong. I had a plan. I was going to tell her."

"Sure you were," his cousin said on a snort of laughter.

"If there's something funny about this," Rafe muttered, "I wish you'd share it. Because I just don't see it."

"I know." Cordell took a long pull of his beer and looked into the mirror, meeting Rafe's gaze with a smile. "And that's the funniest part. Man, if your brothers could see you now."

"You want to step outside and finish that fight?"

"Nope," Cordell said, "and hitting me won't change a thing for you anyway."

"Meaning?"

"Meaning, you're in love with her." Cordell laughed, took another drink of his beer and shook his head. "Another King bites the dust."

"You're wrong." Rafe looked into the mirror, met his own gaze and assured himself that Cordell couldn't have been more wildly off base. He wasn't in love. Had no wish to be in love.

Which was a good thing, he decided grimly. Since the only woman who might have changed his mind about that now wanted nothing to do with him.

Eleven

Katie spent the next few days buried in work.

There was simply nothing better for taking your mind off your problems then diving into baking. She devoted herself to building cookie cakes, decorating birthday cookies and churning out dozens of her clients' favorites.

The scents of cinnamon, vanilla and chocolate surrounded her, giving her a sense of peace that actually went nowhere toward calming her. Inside, her heart was torn and her mind was still buzzing with indignation and hurt. In her dreams, she saw Rafe's face, over and over again, as he looked at her and said, "I can explain." She saw Cordell laughing, Rafe furious and herself, shattered.

He'd said she was "important" to him. As what? A means to winning a bet? As a personal challenge to change her mind about the Kings? And if she was so important to him, why hadn't he tried to talk to her since that night? Why had he been able to let her go so easily?

God, she wasn't making sense. She didn't want him back, did she? So why should she care that he wasn't calling? Wasn't coming over?

Again and again, she relived that night and each time the images danced through her brain, the pain she felt ratcheted up another notch. Her own fault, she knew. She had trusted. Big mistake. She had known going in that she should keep her distance from Rafe. Instead though, she'd followed her heart again, choosing to forget that that particular part of her anatomy was fairly unreliable.

"How many times are you going to go over this anyway, Katie?" she murmured. Shaking her head grimly, she boxed up a dozen chocolate-chip cookies and tied the pink and white striped container with a cotton-candy-colored ribbon.

No matter what else was happening in her life, at least her business was surviving. Thriving, even. The stacks of boxes waiting to be delivered gave her a sense of accomplishment and pride. And that was exactly what she needed at the moment.

This temporary kitchen was her solace. Here she could remember who and what she was. Remind herself that she was building a future for herself. And if that future didn't involve Rafe Cole—she frowned and mentally corrected, Rafe *King*—she would find a way to deal with it.

While the latest batch of cream-cheese cookies baked, Katie wandered to the windows and looked out at the backyard. It was slowly returning to what it had once been. The piles of discarded flooring and plasterboard were gone. Blue tarps covering the grass had been folded and stored away in the crew's trailer, with only squares of dried grass to mark where they had been. The crew was nearing the end of the job and Katie's heart ached at the thought. Her last connection to Rafe was quickly dissolving.

Despite her determination to be strong and self-sufficient, a small, whiny part of her wanted to see Rafe again. Didn't seem to care that he had lied to her. Repeatedly. There was still a dull pain wrapped around her heart and she knew instinctively that it wouldn't stop hurting any time soon.

She hadn't seen Rafe since that night at the restaurant. Apparently his "bet" with Joe had ended the moment she discovered the truth. Rafe had simply walked away without a backward glance, as far as she knew, and it didn't look as though he'd be back. Really, it was as if he had never been here at all, she thought, watching Steve and Arturo carry in the last of the newly refinished cabinet doors.

Katie had walked through her kitchen only that morning in the pre-dawn silence. The pleasure she would have taken in the remodel was muted by the absence of the man who was taking up far too many of her thoughts.

The kitchen was exactly as she had pictured it. The tile floors and granite countertops were in place. All that was left was the finishing work. A few more doors, installing the new drawer pulls and light fixtures, and then her house would be hers again. The crew would leave and she would be alone, with no more contact with King Construction.

Or Rafe.

That twinge of pain twisted in her chest again and

she wondered if it would always be a part of her. She sighed and so didn't hear a thing when Joe entered the patio kitchen.

"Katie?"

She whirled around, startled, to face the man who had been a part of what she now thought of as the Great Lie. He looked uncomfortable, as he had since discovering that she now knew the truth.

Her voice was cool, but polite. "Hello, Joe."

She actually saw him flinch. Though Rafe hadn't been around, she knew that he had been in contact with Joe to tell him that the jig, so to speak, was up.

He shifted position as if he were nervous. "Just wanted to let you know your new stove will be delivered and installed tomorrow morning."

"That's good, thanks."

"The inspector's signed off on everything so we'll move the refrigerator back into the kitchen this afternoon."

"All right." It was almost over, she thought. She wouldn't spend another day cooking in her temporary kitchen. The batch of cookies in the oven now would be the last she baked in her old stove.

"And," he continued, "the guys will be here to help the installers. Then they'll do the last of the finishing jobs and we'll be out of your hair by tomorrow afternoon."

"Okay."

Katie tucked her hands into the pockets of her jeans and as she stood there watching Joe in his misery, she almost felt sorry for him. None of this was his fault. The morning after that scene at the restaurant Joe had explained what had happened and all about the bet Rafe had lost to him.

He'd apologized for going along with Rafe's lies,

but Katie knew he also hadn't had much choice in the matter, either. As an employee, he could hardly argue with the boss. With that thought in mind, she managed to give the man a small smile.

"I have to admit, I'm looking forward to getting my life back," she said. She wouldn't confess to missing Rafe. Not to Joe. Not to anyone.

"Yeah," he muttered, voice still gloomy. "I'll bet."

She noticed he was crumpling an invoice in one tight fist and asked, "Is that the last one?"

He looked down at the paper as if surprised to see it. Then he smoothed it out before holding it out to her. "Your last payment includes the little extras you asked for along the way that were off contract."

Katie nodded and walked over to take it. She didn't even glance at the total. "I'll have a check for you tomorrow."

"That'll be fine." He turned to leave, then stopped and looked at her again. "I'm really sorry, Katie. About everything."

She flushed and now it was her turn to be uncomfortable. Blast Rafe King for putting her in this position. "It wasn't your doing."

"It was, in a way," he insisted, apparently unwilling to let it go that easily. "You know, Rafe's actually a good guy."

"Of course you'd say that," she told him with a sad smile. "You work for him."

"I do," Joe argued, animation coming into his face at last as he tried to defend his employer. "And that's why I'm in a position to know just what kind of man he is. You can tell a lot about a person in the way they treat the people around them. Rafe's not an easy man, but he's a fair one."

"To whom?" Only moments ago, she'd been feeling sympathetic toward Joe since Rafe had put him in such an awkward position. But now, outrage began to bristle inside her. "Was it fair to lie to me? To force you to go along with the lie?"

Joe scowled and scrubbed one hand over his jaw. "No, it wasn't. But he was paying off his bet to me, so I think we should cut him some slack. Not all employers would have had the spine to honor the debt like that."

"Honor?" A burst of laughter shot from Katie's throat.

"Yeah," he said flatly. "Honor. I don't know what happened between you two and I don't want to know. But I can tell you that Rafe's not a man who goes out of his way to treat people badly."

"Just a happy accident, then?" she sniped and instantly regretted it when Joe winced. Honestly, why was she taking her anger and hurt out on him? He hadn't done anything to her beyond supporting Rafe's lies. It was Rafe who had set everything in motion. Rafe who had slept with her and *still* lied to her. Rafe who had let her believe that something amazing was coming to life between them, all the time knowing that it was a sham.

Katie struggled for control and found it. Forcing a smile she didn't feel, she said, "Joe, why don't we just call this a draw and agree not to talk about Rafe King?"

A moment or two passed when it looked as though he might argue with her. But at last, Joe nodded in surrender. "That's fine, then. I'll just let you get back to work and go see if I can help the boys finish up any faster."

She watched him go, then took a deep breath and tried to push Rafe from her mind. Again.

Naturally, it didn't work.

It had been almost a week since he'd last seen Katie Charles.

Rafe felt like a caged man. He was trapped in his own memories of her no matter what he did to try to shake them loose. Her image haunted his dreams, and awake, he couldn't seem to keep thoughts of her at bay. Didn't matter where he was or what he did, Katie was never more than a thought away.

Hell, he'd even considered calling one of the women he knew, to dive back into his life. Get back in the normal swing of things. But damned if he'd been able to make himself do it. No, he had a charity event he had to go to in a few days, but until then, he wasn't going out.

Didn't have the patience to put up with any of the women he knew and wasn't interested in finding someone new.

He just wanted to be alone. But not by himself. Which didn't make sense even to him.

He had tried holing up in his suite at the hotel, locking himself away with only his racing brain to keep him company. But the hotel rooms felt sterile, impersonal, and the echoing emptiness had pounded on him until he thought he might lose what was left of his mind.

So here he sat, trying to focus on inventory and supply sheets while images of Katie taunted him. To make matters worse, there was Sean. The problem with coming into King Construction offices, Rafe told himself, was that he couldn't really avoid his brothers.

"What is your problem?" Sean asked.

"I'm fine," Rafe insisted, keeping his head down, his gaze on the paperwork scattered across his desk. "Just get off my back, all right?"

Sean laughed. "Trust me when I say, I'd love to. But you're making everyone around here nuts. When Janice was doing some phone work for me, she *begged* me to get you out of the office."

That's great, he thought. Always before, Rafe had kept his personal and business lives separate. Now though, it seemed his lousy attitude was bleeding into the office. Hell, maybe he should take some time off. But if he did that, his mind would have far too much time to think about Katie. So whether his assistant was happy about it or not, he wasn't going anywhere.

Rafe scowled and looked up to watch his brother stroll around the perimeter of his office. When Sean stopped at a shelf and plucked a signed baseball off its pedestal, Rafe grumbled, "Put that down." When he complied, Rafe demanded, "Why is *my* assistant doing work for you anyway? Don't you have your own? What happened to Kelly?"

Sighing, Sean walked over and perched on the edge of Rafe's desk. "She eloped last weekend."

"That's the third assistant you've lost this year, isn't it?"

"Yeah. I've got to stop hiring the pretty ones," Sean mused. "Inevitably, they run off and get married and leave me swinging in the wind."

"Well, call the temp agency and get someone in here. Just leave Janice alone."

"Funny," Sean said, his eyes narrowing as he watched Rafe thoughtfully, "she'd rather work for me these days."

Disgusted, Rafe muttered, "Yeah, well, she doesn't."

"Better she work for me than quit. And until you lighten up, nobody wants anything to do with you. So why don't you just tell me what's going on?"

"Work," Rafe said flatly, his gaze giving nothing away as he glared at his brother. "You should try it."

"Just so you know? The whole 'King Glare' thing doesn't work on me. I can do it too, remember?"

Rafe tossed his pen to the desktop and, giving into the irritation flooding his system, jumped out of his chair as if he couldn't bear to sit still any longer. Turning his back on his brother, he stared out the window at the spread of sunlit ocean before him. There were a few sailboats out on the water today and in the distance, fishermen lined the pier. Gray clouds gathered on the horizon and the wind whipped the waves into choppy whitecaps.

"So," Sean asked again, "what's going on?"

He glanced back over his shoulder. He knew his younger brother wouldn't go away until he got some answers. And a part of Rafe wanted to say it all out loud anyway, so he blurted, "Found out which King hurt Katie."

"Yeah? Who?"

"Cordell."

"Should have thought of him," Sean mused with a nod. "He goes through women faster than Jesse used to."

At mention of their now-married cousin, Rafe almost smiled. As a former professional surfer, Jesse King's reputation with the ladies had been staggering. Of course, that was before he married Bella and became a father.

"How'd you find out who it was?"

Rafe muttered an oath and looked at Sean. "Ran into Cordell when I took Katie to dinner."

"Ouch." Sean nodded thoughtfully, clearly understanding the situation.

"Yeah. That about covers it." Pushing one hand through his hair, Rafe looked back at the ocean and said, "It all happened pretty fast. I punched him. Then he told Katie who I was. Then she left."

"And you let her go."

Swiveling his head around, he glared at Sean again. "What was I supposed to do? Hold her captive?"

"Or talk to her?"

"She was through talking," Rafe assured him, remembering the look in her eyes as she faced him down. He'd seen the pain glittering brightly in tears she hadn't let fall. He'd heard the betrayal in her voice and felt the sharp sting of his own lies catching up with him.

"So that's it?" Sean asked.

"That's it." Deliberately, Rafe turned his back on the view, ignored his brother and took a seat behind his desk again. Picking up his pen, he stared blindly at the supply sheets.

"Can't believe you're going to let her get away."

"I didn't *let* her do anything," Rafe muttered, still not looking up at Sean. "Katie makes her own decisions. And now she has more reason than ever to hate the Kings. Most especially, *me*."

Blowing out a breath, Sean stood up but didn't leave. "And you're okay with that?"

"Of course I am," Rafe lied and mentally congratulated himself on just how good he was getting at it. "I always intended to walk away from her, Sean. It just happened a little faster than I'd planned."

God, that was a lie, too.

"Right." Sean slapped one hand down on top of the papers, forcing Rafe to look up at him.

"Butt out, Sean," he ground out.

"Hell no," his brother said, frustration simmering in the air between them. "You're not usually a stupid guy, Rafe. But this time, you're being an idiot."

No, he wasn't. Katie didn't want to see him and he couldn't blame her. Besides, it was better this way. If she was mad at him, she wouldn't stay hurt for long. She'd get over it. So would he. He was no good at love and he knew it. Better he hurt her now than destroy her later.

"Thanks for the input." Rafe peeled Sean's hand off the papers. "Now go away."

"If you don't go after her," Sean said quietly, "you'll regret it."

Rafe already regretted it. Enough that his soul felt as if it was withering and his heart could barely summon the energy to beat.

"I've had regrets before," he finally said. "Let's remember Leslie."

"Uh-huh. Speaking of your ex…I hear you hired her husband."

Rafe sighed. Yes, he had hired John. And he was forced to admit that he might not have if he hadn't met Katie. Being with her had allowed him to face his own past. And the talk with Leslie had been eye-opening enough that he'd been able to reach out to an old friend. Maybe he and John would actually be close again someday.

If they were, that too would be laid at Katie's feet. Her optimism and rosy outlook on life had affected him more than he would have thought possible. Rafe shifted in his chair. He didn't want to talk about any of this. Hell, he didn't want to talk at all.

"So the question is," Sean continued, oblivious to the fact that Rafe wanted him gone, "why is it you can make peace with John and Leslie, but you won't go see the woman you're crazy about?"

Several silent, tense seconds passed before Rafe finally asked, "Are you going to leave? Or do I have to?"

"I'll go," Sean said amiably. "But that won't solve your problem for you."

"Yeah?" Rafe countered. "What will?"

Sean laughed at him and shook his head as he opened the door. "You already know the answer to that, Rafe. You just don't want to admit it."

Twelve

"It's really gorgeous, honey," Emily O'Hara said as she walked through the completely remodeled kitchen. "I love the floor and the counters are just beautiful."

Katie should have been cooing over her finished kitchen too, but somehow she couldn't muster up the enthusiasm for it. Heck, in the two days since the crew left, she hadn't even made a single batch of cookies in her shiny new stove.

Her gaze swept the remodeled room, trying to see it as Nana was, from the slate gray tiles to the pearlized blue granite counters to the dark blue walls and she felt... nothing. It was all perfect and it meant... nothing.

"All right, sweetie," her grandmother said, coming up to give her a brief, comforting hug. "You've got the kitchen of your dreams, but you're standing there looking as if you just found out cookies had been banned. Tell me what's wrong."

The tears that Katie had been holding at bay for days crested again and before she could stop them, one or two trailed down her cheeks. Her heart ached and it felt as though there were a boulder sitting on her chest. She could hardly draw a breath without wheezing. "Oh, Nana, *everything's* wrong."

"Honey…" The older woman sighed and steered Katie across the room. An ancient, round pedestal table and captain chairs sat before the wide window where sunlight splashed and curtains danced in a soft wind. Emily pushed her granddaughter into one of the chairs, then sat down beside her. "Talk to me."

Where to start? Katie wondered. With the fact that she was in love with a man she didn't really know? That she'd allowed herself to get bamboozled by the King family? *Again?* Or should she just admit that she wasn't getting over it this time? That she would *never* get over it? That she couldn't sleep, she couldn't eat, she didn't even want to bake anymore. And that was saying something. She just couldn't bring herself to care about anything but the gaping hole in her own heart.

"It's Rafe," she said, slumping back into her chair. "He lied to me."

"I know."

"What?" Katie blinked at her grandmother and waited for an explanation. But the older woman just sat there in the sunlight, smiling benevolently. "How? What? How?"

Emily reached over, patted Katie's hand, then sighed and leaned back in her chair. "I know his real name is Rafe King, if that's what you're talking about."

"Well, yeah, it is."

"Do you want tea? We should have some tea."

"I don't want tea," Katie said, stopping her grandmother before the woman could get up. "I want some answers. You know about Rafe? For how long?"

She waved one hand dismissively. "Oh, I knew the minute you introduced us."

"How?" Katie just stared at her in rapt confusion. "Do you have some kind of inner lie radar that I didn't get?"

"No, and I don't think I'd want it, either. Sometimes lies can be a good thing," Emily said, her gaze locked on Katie.

"Lying is *not* a good thing. You're the one who taught me that, remember?"

Again, Emily waved a hand, effectively wiping away that little nugget of so-called wisdom. "That was different. You were ten. Now you're an adult and surely you've learned that sometimes a small, harmless lie is far better than a hurtful truth."

"This lie wasn't harmless," Katie argued, remembering the sting of betrayal when she'd discovered Rafe's game. "And you still haven't told me how you knew who he was."

"If you read popular magazines once in a while, you would have known him too," Nana said with a huff. "There's always one King or another's picture in there. I recognized Rafe from a picture taken at a movie premiere."

"A premiere." Katie shook her head and felt her heart drop through the floor. He was used to dating actresses and going to fabulous parties. Oh, he must have gotten such a laugh from the spur-of-the-moment barbecue in her backyard.

Annoyance flickered into anger and soon that hot little bubble of fury was frothing into real rage. "I can't believe it. He must have thought I was an idiot for not recognizing him." She paused for a glare at her grandmother. "And why didn't you *tell* me?"

"Because," Emily said. "You needed your life shaken up a little. Besides, he's a cutie-patootie and you can't hang *all* of the Kings for what one of them did."

"*Two* of them now," Katie reminded her.

"All right, yes, Rafe's not looking too good at the moment," Emily admitted. "But did you give him a chance to explain?"

"Oh, he explained. I was a bet gone wrong."

"Katie…"

She shook her head and held up both hands. "No, Nana, there's no excuse for what he did. He lied to me and that's it."

"I lied to you too, sweetie," her grandmother pointed out in a small voice.

Sighing, Katie said, "Yeah, but you didn't do it to hurt me."

"No, I didn't. And maybe that wasn't Rafe's intention, either."

"We'll never know, will we?" Katie muttered, as anger seeped away into the wide black hole she seemed to be carrying around inside her these days.

"You could find out if you'd stop hiding away in your house and go see him." Emily frowned and looked at her steadily. "Are you really going to become a hermit while he's out having a good time?"

That caught her attention quickly enough. Rafe was having a good time? Where? And a moment later the more important question—*with who?*—leaped into mind.

"What do you mean?" Katie asked, voice tight.

Her nana sighed again and reached for the morning paper, still folded and unopened on the kitchen table.

"Honestly, Katie, if you paid a little more attention to current events…"

"What does that have to do with anything?"

Silently, Emily discarded the news section and went straight to Lifestyles. Thumbing through it, she finally found what she was looking for and folded it back. Then she laid it down in front of Katie and stabbed a grainy black-and-white picture with her manicured nail. "It means, you can find out a lot by keeping up with gossip. Like for example…there."

Katie looked at the picture and felt the tightening in her chest ratchet up until she couldn't get any air in her lungs. She was light-headed. That had to be the reason her vision was narrowing until all she could see was the picture in the paper. The picture of an unsmiling Rafe in a tuxedo at a charity fundraiser, with a blond sporting boobs twice the size of Katie's clinging to his arm.

"When was—" She broke off as she read the caption under the photo. "Two nights ago."

"*He's* not curled up in the fetal position like someone else I could mention," Emily murmured.

"That rat. That *creep*." Katie slowly rose from her chair, clutching the paper in her fists. Her gaze still locked on the picture, all she could see was Rafe's face, glaring at the camera as if he were wishing the photographer into the darkest bowels of Hell.

"Atta girl," her grandmother whispered.

"He told me I was *important* to him," Katie said, fury coloring her voice until it quivered and shook with the force of it. "He must have been lying *again*. If I was so damn important, how is he out with this bimbo?"

"To be fair, we're not sure she's a bimbo," Nana said.

Katie glared at her. "Whose side are you on?"

"Right."

"Does he think I'm stupid?" Katie asked, not waiting for an answer. "Did he really believe I wouldn't find out that less than a week after—after—that he'd be dating the rich and pointless again? Does he think I don't read the paper?"

"Well," Emily pointed out easily, "you don't."

"I will from now on," Katie promised, giving the paper a hard shake.

"So, what're you going to do about this?"

Katie finally lifted her gaze and looked into her grandmother's eyes. With cold, hard determination she said simply, "I'm going to go dethrone a King."

Rafe couldn't settle.

He felt uncomfortable in his own skin.

Which left him nowhere to run.

Not that he would. Kings didn't run. Kings didn't hide.

But then if that were true, why wasn't he over at Katie's house right now, demanding she listen to him? Grumbling, he stood up, walked to the window of his office and stared out at the view without even seeing it. The ocean could have dried up for all the notice he gave it. There might as well have been empty sand dunes stretching out into eternity out there. He didn't care. It didn't matter. Nothing did.

He'd tried going back to his life, but it was a damned empty one. Hell, he couldn't even go into his hotel suite anymore. The silence was too much to take. So instead, he stayed here. At the office. He'd been sleeping on the damn couch, if you could call it sleep.

Every time he closed his eyes, he saw Katie, as she had been that last night. Quivering in his arms. Kissing him breathless. Then finally, staring at him out of hurt-filled eyes. And if he had been able to figure out how to do it, he'd have punched his own face in days ago.

The intercom buzzed and he walked to stab a finger at the button. "Damn it, Janice, I told you I didn't want to be disturbed."

"Yes, but there's—" she said, then added, "Wait! You can't go in!" just before his office door crashed open.

Katie stood in the doorway, her green eyes flashing at him dangerously. Her hair was a wild tumble of curls around her shoulders. She wore a black skirt, a red button-down shirt that was opened enough that he could see where her silver necklace dipped into the valley of her breasts. And she was wearing those black high heels she'd been wearing their last night together.

Altogether, she looked like a woman dressed for seduction. But with the fury in her eyes, any man she was aimed at might not survive. Rafe was willing to take his chances. And if she did end up putting him down, he couldn't think of a better way to go.

"Sorry," Janice was saying as she brushed past Katie with a frown. "She got past me and—"

"It's okay, Janice. Close the door on your way out."

"Yes sir," she said and, though curiosity was stamped on her face, she did what he asked and left he and Katie alone.

"It's good to see you," he said, knowing that for the understatement of the century.

"It won't be in a minute," Katie promised and stalked toward him like an avenging angel on a mission. She dipped one hand into the black purse hanging off her shoulder and came back up with a folded newspaper.

Once she had it, she threw it at him. He caught it instinctively and gave it a quick glance. Ah. Now he knew what was behind the fresh fury driving her. And weirdly, it gave him a shot of hope that she wasn't lost to him completely since that picture had definitely pissed her off.

"Did you think I wouldn't see it?" she said, her voice little more than a snarl. "Or was it just that you didn't care if I saw it? Game over, bet won, moving on? Was that it?"

"It wasn't a game, Katie," he said and his tone was as tight as the tension coiled inside him. "I told you that. Or I tried to."

"And I should believe you," she said, dropping her purse onto the closest chair and stabbing one finger at the newspaper he tossed to his desk. "Because clearly you missed me so much you had to rush out and drown your sorrows in that blonde double D."

He grinned at her, even knowing that would only feed the flames of her wrath. Rafe couldn't help himself. Hell, he could hardly believe she was standing here. Even gloriously furious, she was the only woman who could make his heart lift out of the darkness he carried inside him. The only woman who made him want to smile. Who made him want to promise her any damn thing she wanted as long as she never left him again.

He thought briefly about what Cordell had said at the restaurant the other night. *Another King bites the dust.* He'd argued the point then, out of sheer stubbornness and a refusal to see the truth for what it was.

But now that Katie was standing here in front of him, bubbling with a fury that had her green eyes flashing like fireworks, he knew he couldn't deny the facts any longer. Not even to himself. More importantly, he didn't want to.

He was in love for the first time in his life.

And damned if he'd lose her.

"Don't you dare laugh at me," she warned.

"Not laughing." Reaching out, he grabbed hold of her shoulders and only tightened his grip when she tried to twist free. "Katie, that blonde is an actress. Under contract to my cousin Jefferson's film company. I had to go to the charity thing anyway and he asked me to escort her to get her some media."

She wasn't mollified. "And I should believe that *why?*"

"Because she was boring and vapid and I had a terrible time because she wasn't you. And…because I won't lie to you again, Katie."

Some of the fight went out of her. The rigidity in her shoulders faded enough that he risked easing his grip on her. She didn't step away from him when she had the opportunity and Rafe silently considered that a good sign.

"I miss you," he said before he could gauge his words and try to predict her reaction.

Her delectable mouth flattened into a grim line. "I'm still furious with you."

"I get that." But she was *here* and he was taking that as a good sign. She looked up at him with those gorgeous green eyes and Rafe knew that he had only this one shot. This one chance to redeem himself. To somehow salvage the most important relationship he'd ever known.

So the words came slowly, but they came.

Words he had never thought to say to anyone.

"I wasn't ready for you," he started and read the confusion in her eyes. "The bet with Joe? It shouldn't have been a big deal. But then I met you and found out you hated the Kings and I knew if I told you the truth, you'd never look at me again."

She frowned, and bit into her bottom lip as if trying to keep herself from talking so that she could hear him out completely.

"I told myself that I wanted to change your mind about the King family," he said and watched a flash of something in her eyes come and go. "But it wasn't only that. Like I said, I knew you'd never look at me again if you knew. And I *wanted* you to look at me, Katie," he said, shifting one hand to cup her cheek. "I wanted a lot more than that, too."

"You got more, Rafe," she said, her voice so quiet he had to strain to hear her. "You got more than I ever gave anyone before. I *loved* you. So when I found out you had lied to me, it hurt far deeper than anything Cordell made me feel."

"I know," he told her, mentally holding fast to the word *loved*. If she had loved him then, she had to love him still. It couldn't burn out that fast, no matter how angry she was. "I know."

He pulled her close and kissed her once, twice. It was soft and hard, passionate and tender. That one kiss carried his heart and he nearly sighed in relief when she leaned into him to return that kiss, however hesitantly she did it.

Pulling back, he let his gaze move over her features, as if burning this moment, her expression, into his brain. Finally though, he drew away and said, "I told you I wasn't ready for you and that's the honest truth. But I don't know how I could have been prepared for what you would do to me."

"Rafe…"

He shook his head and laid his fingertips over her

mouth. "No, let me say it. You grew up with your grandmother, your mom. You knew you were loved and you knew how to respond to it. I didn't. My dad was a lousy role model and I hardly knew my mother. When I got married, it was for all the wrong reasons and when she left, my ex let me know that it was *my* failings, my inability to love, that ruined everything—"

Katie's eyes shone brightly as she reached up to smooth her palm across his jaw. "She was wrong."

"No," he said, "she wasn't. Because until I met you, I didn't know how to love."

"Oh, Rafe…"

His heart felt light for the first time in days. His soul was warm again because she was near. Rafe knew that this one woman was the center of his world. If he couldn't convince her to take a chance on him—to love him in spite of all the reasons she shouldn't—then he'd never have anything worth a damn.

"Look, I'm a bad bet," Rafe told her, determined to be completely honest with her even if it cost him what he wanted most. "I know that. But I love you, Katie. In my whole life, I've never loved anything else."

Tears glittered in her eyes and his stomach hitched. Happy tears? Or goodbye?

She took a breath, let it slide from her lungs and admitted, "I want to believe you."

Rafe smiled and pulled her in close to him, where she could feel the hammering of his heart in his chest. Where she would feel the strength of his love wrapping itself around her.

"Take a chance on me, Katie," he whispered, dipping his head to kiss the curve of her neck. He inhaled the scent of her and smiled as cinnamon and vanilla surrounded him. "I swear you'll never regret it."

"Rafe?"

He pulled back to look into her eyes and before she could speak again he said, "Marry me, Katie. Marry me and let me live with you in that great old house. Let me make you happy. I know I can. I'll prove to you that I can be what you need."

"Yes, I'll marry you." Finally, a slow smile curved her mouth and she reached up with both hands to cup his face between her palms. "Don't you know that you're *already* everything that I need?"

"Thank God," he whispered and kissed her again, a promise of more to come.

"After all, you did build me a nearly perfect kitchen."

"Nearly?" he asked with a grin.

"Well, I've suddenly decided that since I'm marrying a carpenter, he should be able to build me a pantry."

"Anything you want, Katie," he promised with a grin. "But I warn you, as soon as he finds out we're getting married, my brother Sean's going to want cookies."

"For family?" she said, *"Anything."*

Rafe dropped his head and rested his forehead against Katie's, feeling his world, his life slide into place again. The woman he loved was in the circle of his arms, and the future was suddenly looking bright. He was right where he wanted to be. Where he was supposed to be.

With Katie Charles, the cookie queen.

Epilogue

Katie grinned as she looked out the kitchen window at her crowded backyard. "I never dreamed there were so many Kings in California."

Julie King, married to Travis, laughed as she pulled a bowl of pasta salad from the fridge. "And this isn't all of them by any means."

"Wait until your wedding," Maggie King, wife of Justice warned her. "They'll *all* be there for that."

"Yep," Jericho's wife Daisy agreed. "They never miss a wedding. Jeff and Maura will even come in from Ireland for that."

"It's a little intimidating," Katie admitted, unwrapping a platter of cookies designed especially for their engagement party. There were dozens of golden crowns, frosted in yellow or white, with Katie and Rafe inscribed on them.

She glanced down at the emerald engagement ring

glittering on her finger and almost hugged herself just to make sure she was awake and not dreaming all of this. But remembering the night before, when Rafe had made love to her for hours and then held her as she slept was enough to convince her that yes. Her life really was perfect.

It had been a month since she'd stormed her way into his office and he laid siege to her heart with the truth. And in that time, she hadn't once regretted taking a chance on Rafe. He'd shown her in countless little ways just how important she was to him. He'd built her that specially designed pantry just as he'd promised. He sent her flowers, made her dinner and when she was tired, he gave her a fabulous foot rub that inevitably led to long, lovely hours in bed.

"Uh-oh," Daisy said with a laugh. "I know that smile."

"What?" Katie grinned, embarrassed to be caught daydreaming.

"It's the same one I get when I remember how I ended up with a gorgeous baby girl." Standing up, Daisy smiled. "And speaking of Delilah, think I'll just go and make sure Jericho's not teaching her how to do something dangerous. The man's got a thing about his daughter being the first female Navy SEAL."

"I know how she feels," Ivy King said, rubbing a rounded belly. "Tanner already plans on our poor baby being the next computer genius of the universe. But no pressure."

As Daisy left and the other King wives laughed and chatted about their kids and their husbands, Katie took a minute to enjoy where she was. Her nana had been right all along of course. Which Emily had continued to remind her of over the last month. Love was worth taking a chance on. Because Katie had risked it, she was about to marry the man she loved, become a part of a huge family and, one day, start her own.

Babies. They would come soon. Rafe had already talked about how he wanted to add to the next generation of the King family.

"It's funny," Katie said softly to the women who were already her friends as well as almost-relatives. "Just a few months ago, I hated the Kings."

"Yeah," Jackson's wife Casey said as she unwrapped a sheath of plastic cups, "we all heard about Cordell. If it helps, everyone knows he's a dog."

Maggie chimed in with, "Justice offered to beat him up, as soon as Cordell arrived today, but apparently Rafe already took care of it."

"Yeah, he did," Katie assured them. "But as much as I hate to admit it, without Cordell being a jerk, I might never have fallen in love with Rafe."

"So, it was worth it then?" Jesse's wife Bella asked.

"More than," Katie assured them. Then she glanced out the window to see her neighbor Nicole walking into the yard with her son in tow. "A friend of mine just showed up. I'll be back to finish up the potato salad!"

"No, you won't," Julie told her. "This is *your* engagement party. Go out and enjoy it. We'll take care of the setup."

Smiling, Katie left her beautiful kitchen and walked into the yard. Her grandmother and aunt were in heaven, playing with all of the King kids. The men were gathered around the brick barbecue Rafe had finished building only last week, arguing over the best way to grill steaks. She caught a glimpse of Rafe in the middle of them all and couldn't help smiling. She had been so wrong. The rich weren't snobby. At least, the Kings weren't. They were just people.

"This is some party," Nicole said as she walked up and gave Katie a hug.

"It is. And I'm so glad you came."

"Wouldn't have missed it. As your future matron of honor, it's my duty to sit here and have a beer and eat steak." Nicole picked Connor up and placed him on her hip. "And your ring bearer wants a cookie."

Katie laughed, delighted, and leaned in to kiss Connor. "My special ring bearer can have as many cookies as I can sneak him!"

When two strong, familiar arms snaked around her middle from behind, Katie leaned back into Rafe's chest with a sigh of satisfaction.

"Hi, Nicole," he said, planting a quick kiss on Katie's head. "Glad you could make it."

"Are you kidding? Wouldn't be anywhere else," she told him. Then with a wry smile at the two of them, she added, "I'll just take Connor in to grab a cookie. We'll see you later."

Rafe turned her to face him and Katie flung her arms around his neck. He kissed her hard and long and deep and when her head was buzzing and her balance had completely dissolved, he lifted his head and looked down at her. "Have I told you today how much I love you?"

"You have," she said, "but I never get tired of hearing it."

"Good. I plan to say it often. Just so you never forget it."

"Not a chance," she promised.

He rested his forehead against hers. "So, after meeting the thundering herd of Kings, you still want to marry me next month?"

His tone was joking, but she knew that a part of him

was still worried that something might happen to tear them apart. He might not believe that he was capable of love, but Katie knew differently. Rafe King had more love to give than most men, simply because he'd never known it before. And she knew that once his heart was given, it was forever.

"You're not getting away from me now, Rafe," she said softly. "We're getting married and I am going to love you forever."

His eyes flashed, his mouth curved, and he pulled her in hard against him for a hug that left her breathless. But who needed to breathe when you were surrounded by love?

When he finally let her go, he draped one arm around her shoulders and, together, they walked into the circle of family.

* * * * *

COMING NEXT MONTH

Available June 14, 2011

You can find more information on upcoming
Harlequin® titles, free excerpts and more at
www.HarlequinInsideRomance.com.

REQUEST YOUR FREE BOOKS!
2 FREE NOVELS PLUS 2 FREE GIFTS!

Harlequin® *Desire*

ALWAYS POWERFUL, PASSIONATE AND PROVOCATIVE

YES! Please send me 2 FREE Harlequin Desire® novels and my 2 FREE gifts (gifts are worth about $10). After receiving them, if I don't wish to receive any more books, I can return the shipping statement marked "cancel." If I don't cancel, I will receive 6 brand-new novels every month and be billed just $4.05 per book in the U.S. or $4.74 per book in Canada. That's a saving of at least 15% off the cover price! It's quite a bargain! Shipping and handling is just 50¢ per book in the U.S. and 75¢ per book in Canada.* I understand that accepting the 2 free books and gifts places me under no obligation to buy anything. I can always return a shipment and cancel at any time. Even if I never buy another book, the two free books and gifts are mine to keep forever.

225/326 SDN FC65

Name _____ (PLEASE PRINT)

Address _____ Apt. #

City _____ State/Prov. _____ Zip/Postal Code

Signature (if under 18, a parent or guardian must sign)

Mail to the **Reader Service:**

IN U.S.A.: P.O. Box 1867, Buffalo, NY 14240-1867
IN CANADA: P.O. Box 609, Fort Erie, Ontario L2A 5X3

Not valid for current subscribers to Harlequin Desire books.

Want to try two free books from another line?
Call 1-800-873-8635 or visit www.ReaderService.com.

* Terms and prices subject to change without notice. Prices do not include applicable taxes. Sales tax applicable in N.Y. Canadian residents will be charged applicable taxes. Offer not valid in Quebec. This offer is limited to one order per household. All orders subject to credit approval. Credit or debit balances in a customer's account(s) may be offset by any other outstanding balance owed by or to the customer. Please allow 4 to 6 weeks for delivery. Offer available while quantities last.

Your Privacy—The Reader Service is committed to protecting your privacy. Our Privacy Policy is available online at www.ReaderService.com or upon request from the Reader Service.

We make a portion of our mailing list available to reputable third parties that offer products we believe may interest you. If you prefer that we not exchange your name with third parties, or if you wish to clarify or modify your communication preferences, please visit us at www.ReaderService.com/consumerchoice or write to us at Reader Service Preference Service, P.O. Box 9062, Buffalo, NY 14269. Include your complete name and address.

HDES11

Harlequin® Blaze™ brings you
New York Times *and* USA TODAY *bestselling author*
Vicki Lewis Thompson with three new steamy titles
from the bestselling miniseries SONS OF CHANCE

Chance isn't just the last name of these rugged
Wyoming cowboys—it's their motto, too!

Read on for a sneak peek at the first title,
SHOULD'VE BEEN A COWBOY

Available June 2011 only from Harlequin® Blaze™.

"THANKS FOR NOT TURNING ON THE LIGHTS," Tyler said. "I'm a mess."

"Not in my book." Even in low light, Alex had a good view of her yellow shirt plastered to her body. It was all he could do not to reach for her, mud and all. But the next move needed to be hers, not his.

She slicked her wet hair back and squeezed some water out of the ends as she glanced upward. "I like the sound of the rain on a tin roof."

"Me, too."

She met his gaze briefly and looked away. "Where's the sink?"

"At the far end, beyond the last stall."

Tyler's running shoes squished as she walked down the aisle between the rows of stalls. She glanced sideways at Alex. "So how much of a cowboy are you these days? Do you ride the range and stuff?"

"I ride." He liked being able to say that. "Why?"

"Just wondered. Last summer, you were still a city boy. You even told me you weren't the cowboy type, but you're…different now."

HBEXP0611

He wasn't sure if that was a good thing or a bad thing. Maybe she preferred city boys to cowboys. "How am I different?"

"Well, you dress differently, and your hair's a little longer. Your face seems a little more chiseled, but maybe that's because of your hair. Also, there's something else, something harder to define, an attitude…"

"Are you saying I have an attitude?"

"Not in a bad way. It's more like a quiet confidence."

He was flattered, but still he had to laugh. "I just admitted a while ago that I have all kinds of doubts about this event tomorrow. That doesn't seem like quiet confidence to me."

"This isn't about your job, it's about…your…" She took a deep breath. "It's about your sex appeal, okay? I have no business talking about it, because it will only make me want to do things I shouldn't do." She started toward the end of the barn. "Now, where's that sink? We need to get cleaned up and go back to the house. Dinner is probably ready, and I—"

He spun her around and pulled her into his arms, mud and all. "Let's do those things." Then he kissed her, knowing that she would kiss him back, knowing that this time he would take that kiss where he wanted it to go. And she would let him.

Follow Tyler and Alex's wild adventures in
SHOULD'VE BEEN A COWBOY
Available June 2011 only from Harlequin® Blaze™
wherever books are sold.